The Other Side of the Fence

Ana and the Lilys

BY CORINDA EDEVOLD

DORRANCE
PUBLISHING CO
EST. 1920
PITTSBURGH, PENNSYLVANIA 15238

Dorrance Publishing Co
585 Alpha Drive
Pittsburgh, PA 15238
Visit our website at *www.dorrancebookstore.com*

ISBN: 978-1-6386-7289-0
eISBN: 978-1-6386-7640-9

Dedicated To:

My husband Scott and our children, Max, Kenzie, Audrey, Emma, and Oliver.

Inspired By:

Our wonderful children who are so different from one another and so amazing in of each their own way.

Special thanks to my loving husband for encouraging me to write my book.

Contents

Chapter One - Fairies

Bright eyed, Becca asks, "You see them, too?"

I am frozen in shock at what is before me. The walls are made from the most intricate, beautiful stained glass imaginable. Detailed pictures of flowers, animals, stars, and nature glow from the colored glass. Curtains of glowing flowers act as doorways in various locations around the room, and their glow makes the entire space seem warm and magical. But it is not the room of glass or the glowing flowers that have stopped us in our tracks.

In this amazing place, for as far as I can make out, there are fairies filling every space. At least I assume that they are fairies. They look like people, except they are much smaller than us, no taller than a juice box. Sprouting from their backs are wings that are as big as the small creatures themselves and look to be as thin and delicate as spider webs. The creatures are in every color imaginable. One on my left has blue skin with silver wings and is talking with another fairy who has pink skin with matching pink wings. The perfect skin on these creatures have no wrinkles and sparkles in the light, as if they are covered with glitter. Their noses are small and pointy upon their faces while their eyes are very large and round, much larger than human eyes. Their eyebrows are high above their eyes in thin and perfectly arched lines. They are all brightly dressed in the most wonderful, crazy, and colorful outfits imaginable.

I am so mesmerized that I don't realize what is next to me. I jump in surprise as I feel a faint bump on my arm and hear a small voice cry out. Looking to my side, I notice a dainty fairy falling towards the ground. Reaching out quickly, I catch her as gently as I can in my hand and slowly lift her to my face.

"I am sorry; are you alright?" I ask her apologetically.

This must be a dream. *Do I need to apologize in a dream*, I wonder as I regard the magical fairy?

She wears a delicate pink dress that clings to her small body and seems to shimmer and glow. The fabric is so thin that I can make out her silver skin through it. Her long neon-pink hair falls grandly down her back in a soft, shimmery wave.

She slowly sits up and shakes her head, throwing pink glitter in all directions. She unfolds huge silver wings that are covered with a crystal pattern, and with the slightest flutter, they float her into a standing position in my hand.

"What…what is this?" she asks in a sweet and melodic voice while studying my hand. Her large round eyes curiously inspect my hand, then move to my arm, growing even more wide as she does so.

Finally finding my face, her eyes fill with terror, and she suddenly screams, "EEEK!" The small creature quickly flies straight up out of my hand, sending glitter dust in all directions.

"Who are you? What are you? What are you doing here? Where did you come from?" she demands me.

"Are you a real fairy?" I question her dumbly, unable to believe what I am seeing.

Looking bewildered she replies, "Yes, of course I am a fairy."

I release the breath I had been holding and smile widely. "A fairy! I cannot believe this! Who would have thought that fairies were even real?" I ask my sisters Lizzie and Becca.

"Excuse me?" the graceful fairy snaps. I look back at her and notice her hands on her hips and a look of irritation on her face.

"Oh," I mumble slowly. "I am sorry. I didn't mean to offend you."

"Well you did. I am right here. And what else other than a fairy would I be? Surely you don't think I look like a flying troll!"

My face feels hot with embarrassment as I clumsily stammer "I, um, no. No, you do not look like a troll."

Lizzie interrupts me. "I am sorry that my sister insulted you," Lizzie apologizes smoothly while shooting me a look that clearly says I should shut my mouth. "Let's start over," Lizzie continues. "My name is Lizzie, and these are my sister's, Becca and Ana. What is your name?"

Looking cautiously at me, the dainty fairy replies, "My name is Easter." Then after a moment's hesitation, she proceeds curiously, "How did you manage to get here?"

I open my mouth to answer when I become aware that it has become eerily quiet. Pulling my gaze from Easter, I look up to realize that we are surrounded by fairies. The fairies stare at us in amazement with their little mouths open in shock.

They have clustered together and are whispering to each other while keeping their nervous eyes on us. I recognize a steady hum that is growing stronger. Nervously I catch on that even more fairies are coming. There must be a lot more coming, I think, to make such a commotion.

A stream of these delicate creatures begins to come into the room. The small clusters of fairies quickly grow from a few dozen to a few hundred.

I detect the hum behind us as well and twirl around in dismay; we are surrounded. A feeling of panic forms in my chest. *There is nothing to be worried about*, I decide. *They are far too little to hurt us. And fairies are good...right? There is nothing to be afraid of.*

"What do you want?" I ask them, dismayed at the tension that I hear in my voice.

One fairy rises above the rest and glides towards us. She is absolutely stunning with short, curly, purple hair. The top of her dress is strappy and bright yellow with a dark purple belt at her slim waist. Her skirt balloons out over her hips, then slims as it falls around her graceful ankles. The top of her skirt is white, then blends into a vibrant purple by the time it reaches her ankles. There are purple tassels that swing from her belt and a matching purple bag perched upon her delicate shoulders. Addressing us she speaks clearly and without hesitation.

"That is the wrong question. This is our home, and you came here to us. The question is what do YOU want?" With that she plunges her hand into the bag at her side and withdraws a handful of purple dust. Murmuring something so softly that I cannot hear, she swiftly blows the dust towards us.

Screaming out in surprise, I turn and try to run away from the dust. The fairies quickly move out of my way. But before I can escape, an odd feeling overcomes me as the dust covers me. My limbs go limp, and I fall to the floor. Looking to my side, I observe my sisters dropping to the floor also. *What in the world is happening*, I wonder. As I lay there, unable to move, I helplessly watch the fairies approach.

Stay away. I want to scream, but I cannot make a sound. My eyes are heavy, and I cannot keep them open. As my eyes shut, my last thought is, *we should have listened to our parents.*

Chapter Two - Just Me

My name is Ana, and I have two sisters named Lizzie and Becca who are my best friends.

Lizzie is fourteen and has large, intelligent hazel eyes. She is tall and thin and likes to hide her face behind her large glasses. Her face is covered in freckles, and she is always sketching things that she considers beautiful. She especially loves flowers and sits to sketch them whenever she can.

After drawing the flowers, she identifies and names them. Trying to learn as much as she can about how and where they grow. Lizzie likes to know as much as she can about everything, and she aces every test. Even though I am younger, I feel a need to protect Lizzie. She might not be brave, but she is sweet and kind and the smartest person I have ever known.

Becca, on the other hand, is a rowdy eight-year-old. She is athletic, social, and fearless. Her short blond hair is always falling out of a ponytail, and her clear blue eyes are observant and playful. Becca is always up to something; good or bad.

One day she hurt her leg pushing a puppy out of the way of an oncoming vehicle. The next day, she got detention for listening to music in class. She is very competitive and will do something again and again until she masters it. But she is also a good sport, congratulating others when they do well.

Becca is always surrounded by friends, eager to catch a glimpse of what she will do next and willing to follow her into whatever trouble she comes upon. Even though she is younger than me, I find myself following her lead also. She is a natural leader.

I am the middle child at the awkward age of eleven. I fall into the middle category of most things. I go to school and play tennis and sing in the choir. But I am not the star of the tennis team and I do not sing solo in the choir; instead I prefer to blend my voice in with the rest. I am not the fastest, bravest, or smartest in any area. I am not even lucky! I have never won a coloring contest or even a ribbon at the fair! That is right, I have never won ANY ribbon. Not a third or second place and never a first place. Last year I did not even receive a participation ribbon.

When I asked the judges at the fair why I didn't get a participation ribbon for any of my entries, they said that by their records, I had received more participation ribbons than anyone else...EVER. The judges said that they were sure I had more than enough participation ribbons and that they were sure I would not want any more.

I didn't know how to answer, so I just walked away with my head down, tears slowly leaking from my eyes. Once I thought the judges couldn't see me, I threw my entries into the garbage can in frustration. It wasn't until after I got home that I was finally able to think of what I should have said to those judges.

I should have said that they were right, that I don't want a participation ribbon. That just for once I would like a blue first-place ribbon. I could hang it proudly on my wall, and whenever a friend came over, they would admire it and compliment me on my obvious talent.

Becca would have thought of this immediately and said it. And Lizzie...well Lizzie would have won the blue ribbon. Not only do I not win ribbons, but I do not do well when I am put on the spot. My mind goes blank, and when I should have a comeback or a smart answer, I can't think of anything to say. I panic and get red faced with embarrassment. This is not something that I am proud of, and each time I tell myself that next time, next time I will know how to reply.

I may get tongue tied and don't win any ribbons, but I love to read! I read even more than Lizzie. I do not read to learn about things like Lizzie does though. I love to read because of the stories.

In books the main character always knows what to say, and if they work hard enough, everything works out for them. I often daydream about what my life would be like if it was a story in one of my books. I imagine that I would be articulate and quick to respond with the perfect answer to any question. I would be popular, and everyone in school would be my friend. I would go on adventures, and everyone would look to me to know what to do. I would be the fearless hero of every adventure and save my friends and family from all sorts of trouble.

Not to mention that my walls would be covered with first-place blue ribbons that I would have won from the fair. There would be so many ribbons that you wouldn't be able to determine what color the paint is on my walls.

I frown as I come back to reality. I try, but no matter what I do, I am not the best at anything. I do have a few friends, but friends don't come as easily to me as they do for Becca. I get passing grades, but I have to worry about upcoming tests at school, unlike my sister Lizzie. My hair won't even behave in real life. If my life was in a story book, my hair would be perfect and stay exactly where I want it to. Instead my hair frizzes when I want it straight and it is straight when I want it to curl. I am completely unremarkable and normal in every way.

At least that is what I believed until I learned that I was completely wrong. I was wrong about everything.

Chapter Three - The Fence

My sisters and I like to take walks and search for flowers and berries. We have our own game for this, and the rules are simple enough; whoever finds the prettiest flower or the largest berry wins. Walking in the woods one day, we were arguing about who was winning. I had definitely found the largest strawberry, but Becca had found a beautiful flower, which she claimed was better than my berry. Lizzie was listening intently to Becca's reasoning when she suddenly stopped in her tracks.

"What is that?" Lizzie curiously asks, raising her hand to point.

Turning I spot a white picket fence. It ran right through the woods for as far as I can see. Even though we have been in these same woods numerous times, I had never noticed this before.

Silently we approach the mysterious fence. Surely it had been here all along. We must have just overlooked it. While it was well-cared for and freshly painted, it was not new. In fact the fence looked very old with mature trees and bushes growing alongside it.

I gently place my hands on the wood railings and my fingers slide over them easily. I am surprised by how smooth it is. A warm breeze caresses my face as I shyly peer over the fence.

The sweet smell of flowers greets me, and I am amazed to view a gorgeous meadow. Blooms of all colors sway before me. They are bright, healthy, and perfect and appear to glisten and sparkle in the bright sunlight. I have never seen so many flowers before in my entire life. They are of every shape and size and color imaginable. They are so thick in the meadow that I can barely make out a patch of grass here or there.

Otherwise, it is hidden beneath the flowers.

Hearing a noise, I lift my eyes reluctantly from the lush meadow and gasp in astonishment to see a tall waterfall rushing over a rocky cliff. I squint when the sun blinds me momentarily as it reflects off the water.

Rich green mosses with delicate blue forget me nots decorate the rocks around the waterfall, and vines covered with wisteria drape down on either side of the water from the top of the cliff.

Overcome I sit on the grass and stare at the picturesque scene in front of me. A horse gallops up to the lake and delicately takes a long drink. The horse is tall and strong and sleek. Its white hair shines in the sun, and its thick, silky mane falls luxuriously around its neck. The horse, too, appears to shimmer in the sunlight, and I rub my eyes thinking that my mind must be playing tricks on me. The scene before me flickers and shifts for a moment, as if it might not really be there.

It comes back into focus, and I can clearly distinguish the gorgeous horse flicking its long tail energetically. The horse whinnies as a bevy, or group, of swans fly overhead, then circle and land silently on the water. There are more swans than I have ever seen before, and they are brighter than I remember swans being. The sun reflects blindingly off their white feathers.

Even though they are large, they glide smoothly on top of the water and they splash playfully at the horse. The horse is delighted by this and prances along the bank of the water, neighing and swishing his tail playfully.

Mesmerized I cannot turn my eyes away. Everything seems completely perfect on the other side of the fence. The horse's mane and tail are not tangled, and he shines as if he was just brushed. The flowers are big and bright, the water is clear and clean. The sky is a bright, bright blue. Even the grass looks greener on the other side of the fence than where we are sitting. Sweet fragrances and the warm breeze cross the fence and further hold my attention. I lose all track of time as I admire the perfection on the other side of the fence.

Chapter Four - Forbidden

When it becomes too dark to notice the sparkle in the water, it is as if a spell is broken. Shaking my head, I am astounded to realize my sisters are sitting next to me and that the sun is setting.

"What was that?" I ask aloud. "What just happened?"

My sisters gape at me in stunned silence. Finally, Lizzie blinks her hazel eyes and quietly replies, "I don't know. How long have we been here?"

Becca speaks up, "I don't know either, but I am really freaked out right now."

"Me, too," I agree. "Let's get out of here." Quickly we get up, and I sneak one more look towards the fence as I stand. I am surprised to see the horse watching us. Staring at us intently. Shaking my head in disbelief, I run towards home as fast as I can.

We exit the woods, and I can make out our home in the distance. Our mother is in the front yard. She is tall and slender with jet black hair and dark, dark glittering eyes.

They are darker than brown, a black almost. If I ever meet my grandparents, I would ask them if they named her Night because of her eyes. I don't know what other reason they would have had for giving her such a strange name.

Dad claims it is a beautiful name for our beautiful mother. I do agree that Mother is striking. Her skin is a creamy ivory color and she has bright red, perfect lips. She is prettier than any of the other moms at our school, even though she never wears any makeup. But I still think that Night is a weird name.

As we get closer, I hear her crying out, "GIRLS! GIRLS!"

Spotting us her face lights up with relief, and she begins to rush towards us. Scooping all of us into her arms, we hug tightly as I inhale her sweet, fresh scent. *How does she always smell so lovely*, I wonder. Mother always smells like flowers. I never witness her putting on perfume and I honestly have NO idea where the smell comes from. Nothing else in our home smells like Mother. I don't even know what flower it smells like. I just know that it is the most beautiful scent that I have ever smelled.

Mother suddenly holds the three of us away from her and she scolds, "Where have you been? You should have been back hours ago. Are you alright? What happened?"

Lizzie's elbow is jammed into my side, and Becca's hair gets sucked into my mouth as I try to catch my breath.

"Well?" Mother demands. "Aren't you going to answer me? I was so worried!"

Pushing from her grip, I stammer, "M–M–Mother we found something. "

"Something amazing," Becca adds.

"No, something incredible," Lizzie corrects.

We inform her about the meadow and the waterfall; our words tumbling out in our excitement.

Listening intently Mother's face tightens, and a strange look takes hold of her.

"I don't remember ever seeing the meadow before," I tell Mother. "Can we go back there? Who owns the meadow?" I quiz.

"What?" she stammers in a barely audible whisper.

"Are you okay, Mother? You look pale," I ask her, suddenly concerned.

"We need to talk with your dad. I, I can't believe it," Mother whispers.

"I know it sounds crazy," Becca admits defensively. "But it is true. We saw it."

"I believe what you girls saw. I just can't believe it is here," Mother says distractedly. "Come, come with me," she stutters.

My sisters and I fall silent as we follow her into our home. My mind races. Can't believe it is here? *What does that mean*, I wonder. Should it be somewhere else? It's not like meadows can move! Did Mother know about the meadow already?

Why had she never told us if she knew about it? Or why had we never found it before? I am certain that we have gone there before. In fact I know we have. We built a tree house in that area. I am sure of it! But there was no fence line when we built our tree house. I will check when I go back, I resolve. That cannot be the same spot. I MUST be mistaken.

"What is it? What is wrong?" The concerned voice of my dad pulls me back to reality. I look up to discover him studying us worriedly.

"They saw the meadow," Mother answers in disbelief.

Pulling her moon charm, which she always has on her, from her pocket, she rubs it fiercely with her fingers in anxiety.

"The what? What are you talking about?" Dad asks in confusion.

Raising her head to look Dad in the eye, Mother repeats quietly, "The girls saw the meadow today. The meadow on the other side of the fence!" she exclaims, bursting into tears.

Alarmed, Dad pulls her into his comforting arms. Holding her tightly, realization dawns on his face and he stares at us in horror. Tightening his grip on Mother, Dad looks down at her as she sobs loudly with tears streaming down her ivory face.

"There, there, Night, I have you. Please stop crying," he pleads while patting her hair. Looking back at us, Dad grills, "Did any of you girls cross the fence?"

"What? Why do you ask?" I stammer in confusion.

"What is going on?" Lizzie begs nervously.

"This is important. Did ANY of you cross THAT fence?" Dad demands.

"Uh, no," we each stammer quietly.

Sighing in relief, Dad says, "Thank the Heavens for that." Looking up at the dark sky, Dad is silent but seems to be looking at something intently. Turning around I inspect where he is looking, but all I make out are stars. A black night sky full of beautiful, bright stars and a big full moon. After a moment, Dad lowers his gaze back to us and declares sternly, "No one is to ever go back to that meadow!"

"Stay away from that place. You must never cross the fence," Mother sobs.

"But why? It is so lovely."

"It is forbidden!" Dad snaps harshly. "End of discussion! I don't ever want to hear of any of you girls EVER going back there! Is that understood?"

Shocked that our soft-spoken Dad is snapping at us, I agree quickly, "Yes, Dad."

And I mean it. I will stay away if it means so much to them.

Chapter Five - Temptation

The days go by slowly, and I find myself thinking more and more about the meadow. It looked innocent. *What is my parents' problem?* I wonder. The more I try to put the mystery of the fence and what we saw out of my mind, the more aware I become that I am dwelling on it. I am positive that the fence wasn't there before. But a fence doesn't just appear overnight.

Then what did Mother mean when she said, "It is here," none of this makes any sense to me.

Neither parent mentions it again, and I feel as if they want to forget that we ever had any crazy conversation about a fence suddenly coming out of nowhere.

Except I remember. And I cannot forget, no matter how hard I try. The fence is always on my mind. I dream about the beautiful fence at night. I daydream about what might be on the other side of the fence while I do my chores. I wonder if there are any other animals that frolic in the meadow, and I think of that beautiful horse. I am haunted by the eyes of that horse staring at me as we left the meadow. It was so thoughtful and intelligent. Eerie, I think, as I shudder and turn my attention back to my chores.

"I can't take it anymore," I confess to Lizzie and Becca a few weeks later. "What could be the harm of going back to the fence? I didn't see anything dangerous. Did either of you?"

After a pause, Becca quietly replies, "No. Just beautiful."

"Dad said it was forbidden," Lizzie pipes up. "He has never forbidden anything before, so it must be serious. We should listen to him," she states firmly.

"But every day the urge to return grows stronger and stronger," I plead. "Please come with me. I just can't stand staying away anymore."

"Well," relents Becca, "it wouldn't be too bad of us to go back. Our parents only knew about it because we told them. If we don't tell them that we went back, they won't know."

"But Dad said it was FORBIDDEN," Lizzie reminds us.

"Don't you want to know what those flowers were? I have seen you sketching, Lizzie. And your sketches look like the flowers we saw in that meadow. If we went back, you could get a better look at them," tempts Becca.

"Well," admits Lizzie, "I have been trying to remember what those pink ones looked like. I don't remember ever seeing a flower like that before."

"Just this one time," I plead. "If we notice anything dangerous, we will leave and never go back."

"Okay," Lizzie reluctantly agrees. "Just this one time. What can it hurt to look at some flowers?"

Smiling hugely, I throw my arms around Lizzie.

Jumping up and down, I squeal in excitement, "Thank you, thank you!"

Grabbing Lizzie's hand, then mine, Becca exclaims, "Let's go. Quickly, this way!" Becca commands.

Excitedly we run towards the woods. I steal a glance at Lizzie as we hurry along and am surprised by the huge smile on her face.

Amazed I realize that even Lizzie is excited. *Wow*, I think. *She doesn't get excited about anything.*

As we go deeper into the woods, we slow down, trying to remember the way. Guiltily we look over our shoulders as we go.

Where was it, I wonder. Are we going the right way? "Over there, I see the fence!" Lizzie breathes in disbelief. "I had almost convinced myself that the whole thing had been a dream."

Becca screams in excitement and starts to rush forward.

Squinting through the haze, the glistening meadow comes into my view. As we approach, sheep on the other side of the fence raise their heads and bleat at us. Then calmly return to grazing. Walking along the fence, I find our tree house and am surprised that the fence is directly beneath it. I KNOW we did not build our tree house over the fence.

Something strange is definitely going on here, I think.

Cautiously we climb into our tree house and thoroughly inspect it. Satisfied that our tree house is as it should be, other than having a mysterious fence beneath it that is, we settle down and face the meadow. Sitting in our tree house, my sisters and I relax as we admire the beauty on the other side of the fence. I decide that however strange this fence is, I am glad that we found it.

Chapter Six – Weird Weather

After that we went back to the fence every day. We hauled in our books and read leaning against the fence, listening to the waterfall. We relaxed on the soft grass, enjoying the warm sunlight and lazily reading.

We carefully carried our tea set to the fence and had tea parties. Spreading a blanket on the grass and chatting about the waterfall and our school friends while enjoying treats. We shared our goodies with the animals on the other side of the fence, and when the horse accepted a sugar cube from my hands, I was delighted.

We brought our sketchbooks and tried our best to capture the beauty that we beheld on the other side of the fence. Lizzie, dutifully sketching in detail each of the different flowers. She experimented with multiple packs of colored pencils in different shades, trying to correctly show the vibrant colors. Finally, she brought paints and mixed them to hues that perfectly matched the flowers.

We even did our homework in our treehouse, looking up from time to time to admire the meadow. Then we would force our attention back to our math and English books.

We did everything that we could possibly do at the fence, and we went there as often as we could. It always smelled like flowers and freshly cut grass. The grass next to the fence was as soft as satin, and it was warm by the fence. I know it sounds silly, but it even felt warmer by the fence than elsewhere.

Even on a chilly day, we would arrive bundled up; Lizzie in a sensible rain-proof jacket, Becca in her quick drying athletic wear, and me in a soft, cozy sweatshirt. Soon we would all be warm enough to take off our outerwear. But when we went home, we never got far before we would have to put on our jackets and sweats again.

If the weather was foul, we did not go to the fence. Until one gray, drizzly Saturday, we were indoors and had nothing to do. We reasoned that once we got to the fence, there would be a dry treehouse awaiting us. So, we decided to brave the weather and go.

By the time that we had walked halfway to the meadow, my clothes were soaked. Lizzie had thought to bring an umbrella, so she was dry, but we were all cold. As we came over the hill, arriving at the fence, the rain stopped, and the sun came out. We had a wonderful warm afternoon at the fence. We braided flowers into necklaces while fluffy white sheep and the horse watched us with curiosity. The animals came close to investigate, and we were able to decorate some friendly sheep with our flower jewelry. The adornments didn't last long though because the other sheep quickly and delightedly ate the jewelry as fast as we could make it.

As the sun began to set, we realized that we were hungry and decided to call it a day. On our way home, it began to rain again, and I thought we had been very lucky for the rain to stop for us while we were at the fence.

This all seemed normal until summer turned into fall.

As the leaves began to change color, we noticed that everything on the other side of the fence remained unchanged. The grass maintained its dark green color along with the leaves and the moss. The flowers continued to be vibrant and healthy. The swans never left the lake to migrate south for the winter, and the horse didn't appear to be getting a thicker winter coat.

Surely, I am just imagining things, I decide. Maybe the other side of the fence stays warmer because of the lake. Or global warming or climate change. Though I don't know what the reason is, I am certain that there is a reasonable explanation.

Chapter Seven - For the Birds

Since it was nice fall weather and we normally spent most of our time outside anyway, our parents weren't worried that we might be at the fence. In fact they had never mentioned the fence again. So, my sisters and I never brought it up either.

Our parents obviously knew something about this magical place that they were keeping secret from us. We agreed that coming here would be our secret, and we debated on how to learn more about this mysterious meadow without alerting our parents.

We decided to bring Dad's binoculars with us, so that we could study the meadow and waterfall without crossing the fence. I pressed the binoculars against my eyes and excitedly began to examine the meadow. I focused on the sheep, then the horse before turning my attention to the lake.

How the water glistened in the bright sun. The surface was dotted with green lily pads with bright white flowers in their centers. Tall cattails gently sway in the breeze at the banks of the lake and I notice something else.

I see movement and focus my binoculars on the lily pads. It looked like there were small creatures on them. Some would move from one side of a lily pad to the other. Some flew or hovered above the water. I rubbed my eyes, then I squinted through the binoculars, hoping to make the images clearer.

My first thought was frogs. Frogs live in lakes and ponds. But these creatures were definitely flying or hovering, which frogs cannot do. So they cannot be frogs. *Maybe they are birds,* I wonder. I have never seen birds land on lily pads before, but if they wanted to, I think they could.

One of the small creatures rose high into the air and zipped towards the waterfall. I tried to follow it with my binoculars but lost sight of it in the mist. Wondering where it had gone, I began to study the waterfall closer.

The waterfall was taller than the trees, and it was spectacular how the water rushed over the edge and spiraled down. The water raced towards the lake, splashing and spraying. Mist rose from the impact. It was beautiful. I noticed a small rock sticking through the base of the waterfall, protecting the rocky ground beneath it from the water and keeping it dry.

Suddenly Becca said loudly, "I see something! There, on the dry spot beneath that rock. Do you see it?"

We all looked, and there was something odd there. A small creature was flying in what looked like a circular pattern. Again and again, it flew the same path in the air.

"I have never witnessed any animal fly like that before," Lizzie observes quietly in wonder. "Can either of you make out what it is?"

"Is it a bee maybe?" I ask doubtfully. "Or a dragonfly? Or maybe it is a small bird? I can't make it out it clearly," I admit in dismay.

"Oh. Let's just go investigate!" Becca pleads irritably. "This is silly. Spending so much time wondering when it is right there. Let's just walk over there and check it out."

"No way, Becca," Lizzie pronounces firmly. "We promised…"

She was abruptly cut off as a flock of Blue Jays fly overhead and circle the meadow. There are at least thirty of the brilliant blue birds above us in the clear sky. Noticing them the horse whinnies loudly and stomps his hooves. The sheep look up and then scatter and dash into the woods. Even the swans seem to huddle together on the pond. This is strange behavior, I think. I wonder why the animals are so agitated.

The Blue Jays began to fly towards the waterfall, and the horse gallops quickly in front of them, blocking their path. Screaming loudly the Blue Jays veer off their course and go around the horse. I cover my ears in pain. *What a loud, horrible sound,* I think.

Suddenly my thoughts are interrupted when, from beneath the rock at the base of the waterfall, birds fly out. Fast. I can make out that these creatures are indeed birds. They are little brown birds and they sing and whistle to each other as they rush towards the Blue Jays. Upon sensing the smaller birds, the Jays open their beaks and scream loudly.

My sisters and I duck our heads and cover our ears as we watch in disbelief.

"What is going on?" I ask Lizzie and Becca.

"I don't know, but I recognize those smaller birds as Nightingales. You can always identify them by the songs that they sing," Lizzie states.

"How can you possibly make them out over the Jays?" Becca demands of Lizzie. "I have never heard such a horrible noise before!"

"Blue Jays do make a hideous screech when they are fighting. I have never known Jays to fight with Nightingales before though. In fact, I didn't know that Nightingales even lived in this area. I thought our climate was too cold for them. And I definitely don't remember ever observing them here before," Lizzie concludes as she absentmindedly rubs her chin while studying the birds.

"I don't care what KIND of bird it is; why do they look like they are attacking the Blue Jays? And why did they come out from behind the waterfall? Do they live behind waterfalls normally?" I shout.

"I don't know about that," Lizzie responds. "But I know that they are Nightingales."

The Nightingales cluster together and then charge the other larger birds. The Blue Jays screech one more time then begin to fly away. Upon seeing this, the Nightingales stop and begin to sing in happiness. As a group, they swoop down towards the horse and circle him while singing and whistling. The horse appears to relax and almost looks to smile at the small birds. Continuing to sing in victory, the Nightingales fly back to the waterfall and disappear behind it.

My mouth agape in surprise, I say quietly to my sisters, "I feel like we just watched a battle."

"Birds do NOT battle," Lizzie retorts annoyed.

"Well, what just happened then?" Becca questions her.

"I don't know, but I think we should go home," Lizzie suggests.

Chapter Eight - To Cross or Not to Cross

"Go home!?" Becca shrieks in surprise. "You want to go home after that? No way. The only place that we need to go is behind that waterfall. We need to figure out what is going on."

"Wait, we can't go behind the waterfall," I protest. "We promised our parents that we wouldn't cross the fence."

"So what?" asks Becca. "I mean we are already here."

"Yes, we are here," Lizzie states quietly. "But we agreed that we would leave at the first sign of danger."

"Was that dangerous to you?" Becca interrupts. "We just saw some birds flying. There is nothing dangerous about birds! Especially little singing birds."

"The birds were flying in formation!" Lizzie shouts. "There is something dangerous about that! They were organized."

"Don't be silly, Lizzie," I tell her calmly.

"It was strange how they flew out from behind the waterfall like they did," Lizzie insisted. "They headed straight for the Blue Jays. It was as if they had been notified that there were intruders and they came to chase them away."

"That settles it," Becca declares. "We MUST go and investigate. None of this makes sense. Something is going on here, and I am going to find out what."

"But our parents said to stay away," I reminded her. "And yet here we are. We are already breaking the rules. What would be the difference if we crossed the fence?" Becca challenges.

"Okay," Lizzie relents. "Becca has a point. We have already been coming here, even though we know our parents don't want us to."

"Exactly!" Becca remarks loudly. "Once we cross the meadow and go behind the waterfall, we will KNOW what is there. Come on, you guys!" she pleads. "We are just going right there!" she indicates, pointing towards the waterfall.

"It would be nice if we knew what our parents are hiding from us," I mumble softly. "Mother has acted strangely ever since we mentioned the meadow."

"That's for sure!" Becca agrees. "I found her looking through my drawers the other day. She said that she was putting away my clothes, but there wasn't any clean laundry."

"She read my journal," Lizzie confesses softly. "Not my recent journal. Not the one where I talk about the fence; I have a special place where I keep that journal safe. But I have never known her to read my personal things before."

"Did she say what she was doing?" I ask Lizzie in disbelief. Lizzie has always written in journals ever since she could write, but I have never known of anyone reading them without her permission.

Lizzie looks up sadly and replies, "No. Once she saw me, she just put my journal down and left the room. Rubbing that blasted moon charm of hers the whole time."

We fall quiet as we absorb this information.

"Let's do it," Lizzie concedes. "I think it is time that we figure out what is going on."

We all nod in agreement and carefully and quietly climb over the fence. The sheep come out of the woods and look up as we pass them, then continue to graze. As we near the lake, the horse approaches us and appears agitated.

Neighing and stomping his hooves; he stands between us and the lake.

The horse is tall and muscular. His white hair shines in the sunlight, and he stands towering over us. I look up and see his black nose above my head. His mane hangs in silky waves along his graceful neck as he throws his head from side to side and he looks at us and snorts apprehensively at us.

Cautiously I offer the agitated horse a sugar cube, and after a moment's hesitation, he lowers his nose towards us and carefully sniffs each of us. Suddenly his eyes light up, and the horse whinnies in excitement and quickly takes the treat from my hand.

He looks at us closely as he chews his candy. His contemplation is almost too intent and purposeful for a horse. I feel as if I am being sized up, I think as I shift uncomfortably beneath the horse's steady gaze. Seeming satisfied the horse swings his head to one side and looks towards the waterfall. Slowly we pass by him and approach the waterfall.

Chapter Nine - Where Are We

We reach the waterfall and get down on our hands to knees to look inside the opening beneath the rock. Aware of nothing but darkness, I look at Lizzie and ask, "Are you sure you want to do this?"

"Of course she does!" Becca interrupts as she shoves past us. Becca quickly gets onto her hands and knees and crawls through the opening in the waterfall, disappearing into the darkness.

"Wow, you guys have got to check this out!" she calls back to us. "It is amazing!"

Lizzie and I look at each other uneasily and Lizzie suggests, "After you, Ana."

Taking a deep breath, I put my hands carefully on the slippery wet rock. I feel cool water soak my jeans as I place my knees on the hard ground and slowly begin to crawl forward. It is a cave. I shiver in fear and hope that there are no bats in here with us. Underneath the rock, the waterfall is loud, and as I slowly move forward, it gets darker and I feel a sense of panic.

"Becca," I call out. "Are you okay?"

"For sure!" Becca yells back excitedly. "Just wait until you get a little further, it is... WHOA! What is that!?"

"Are you okay?" I ask her nervously as I pause.

Lizzie's head bumps hard into my butt when I stop suddenly. "Yeah.... hurry up, will you? This is really something."

"You might as well go," Lizzie remarks from behind me. "You know that she won't come out until she shows us."

Slowly I creep forward; further behind the waterfall and I smell something. It is sweet and familiar. I inhale deeply and recognize the scent of lavender, rose, and something else. *Honeysuckle maybe,* I wonder.

Breathing deeply the scent continues to grow stronger, and I relax. Surely whatever is ahead cannot be too bad if it smells like flowers. *It probably isn't bats anyway,* I think cheerily.

I catch a glimpse of light and move faster, feeling relieved to have found the end of the cave. I wonder where this leads. Maybe I will come out on the other side of the meadow. Squinting to see better, I look forward and can make out the light but no Becca. *Now where did she go?* I think in frustration.

I reach the end of the tunnel and stop completely in surprise. Not realizing that I had stopped, Lizzie runs into me from behind and the force knocks me forward.

"Ah!" I scream as I fall out of the cave into the light. My hands slip under me, and my feet flip over my head. *I hope I don't get a bloody nose,* I think as I shut my eyes in fear. I brace myself for falling on the hard rock and I land…softly.

I hear Lizzie gasp and open my eyes. "Am I bleeding?" I demand. "I hate it when I get a cut or a bloody nose…." I stop talking when I realize that I am lying on a thick, soft layer of flowers. I look around quickly and become aware that there are flowers everywhere.

We are not in the meadow like I thought. We are still in the cave, and the damp rock walls are covered with vibrant pink, white, purple, and red roses. Honeysuckles are in bunches, and vines of dainty morning glories zig zag over the walls. Purple wisteria hangs from the ceiling, and I notice Becca gently touching ropes made of dandelions on my right that are holding back curtains of black-eyed susans.

Standing shakily, I am relieved not to be bleeding and I reach down to help Lizzie out of the cave. Her mouth hangs open as she surveys our surroundings. Lizzie stands stupefied and silent. I wave my hand in front of her face to get her attention.

"Are you okay?" I ask her.

"What?" she responds distractedly, not looking at me.

I loudly snap my fingers, and Lizzie finally turns to look at me. I see that her eyes are wide with wonder.

"This is…is…" she stops as if at a loss for how to continue.

Well this is a first, I think. Lizzie doesn't know what to say. I smile at this, relieved to know that my perfect sister can be dumbstruck sometimes. *That is how I am all the time*, I think. Lizzie seems to have forgotten how to walk, so I grab her hand gently and pull her along behind me towards Becca.

When we reach Becca, Lizzie's attention turns towards the ropes also, and she bends down to study them seriously. After a moment, she remarks in awe, "These flowers are alive." Becca and I look at each other in confusion. "Right here," she explains excitedly as she pulls Becca and I closer. "The flowers are all on their stems and are growing from the moss on the walls of the rock. Each dandelion then somehow is sprouting from the previous dandelions, which are then braided around others to form ropes."

"Okay...so what?" asks Becca, rolling her eyes.

"So, no one picked these flowers. No one MADE these ropes; they are growing this way."

As Lizzie slowly tries to separate the dandelions to distinguish better how they are growing from one another, I turn back to the room we are in. There aren't any windows or lamps, but different shades of colors fill the space from all angles. I curiously pick up a delicate bright pink flower that I have never seen before and am startled to observe my hand turn the same bright pink shade as the flower. Peering closer I discover that light is coming from within the flower. The flower is glowing.

Gasping, I drop the flower, and looking around, I realize that all of the light is coming from the flowers.

"How can this be?" I ask in alarm. "Lighted flowers? Curtains and braids of flowers, where are we?"

"I don't know, but this place is amazing," Lizzie reflects in admiration as she gently moves aside some of the wisteria. "Look at this wall-hanging! I have never seen anything like it before."

Turning towards her and stepping closer to investigate, I realize that the flowers are woven together to cover an entire wall.

Different types of flowers are deliberately placed to soften, blend, or harden the lines of the picture. Each individual flower is healthy and perfect and most definitely alive. Like the ropes, these flowers are also somehow growing strategically to form something. I step back to admire the entire picture and I realize that it is of a majestic white Pegasus.

Strong and menacing, the Pegasus is flying through the clouds above the meadow. Delicate purple flowers on green vines decorate the Pegasus. They are woven in its mane and around its neck. They are spectacular flowers, except for one dark, dark brown spot that appears to be emerging from within one of the purple flowers near Pegasus's ear. The Pegasus casts a shadow on the meadow below as it stares intently down. Its eyes are narrowed in focus and its ears are back threateningly.

"Holy cow!" Becca exclaims loudly. "It looks so real!"

"It's magical," Lizzie breathes. "And look at those purple flowers on the Pegasus. They are Nightshade flowers, gorgeous but horribly poisonous."

"The picture looks a little scary," I comment nervously. "The Pegasus looks as if it is hunting something."

"Don't be a scaredy cat," Becca coaxes me playfully. "Pegasus is beautiful, and the wall-hanging is made from flowers. How can something that is made from flowers be scary?" she teases me.

"It still gives me the creeps," I assert as I stare up at the picture and shiver. "Maybe we should go back."

Becca grabs the curtain of black eyed susans and looks at Lizzie and I defiantly. "We came here to find out more about this place. We are going to do just that," she announces bravely as she pulls the curtain wide open.

Looking beyond the curtain, we gasp in wonder. *Surely I am dreaming*, I think. "Do you see this?" I whisper.

"It can't be," Lizzie breathes. "There is no such thing as fairies."

And that is where our story began. Allow me to recap for you.

For as far as I could see, there were fairies filling every space on the other side of that curtain. I was so mesmerized that I was surprised to feel a bump on my arm and hear a small voice cry out. A dainty fairy had crashed into my arm and was tumbling towards the ground. Reaching out quickly, I caught her gently and met my first fairy-Easter.

The other fairies clustered around us whispering. I hate to admit this, but it made me nervous, and I felt a little scared. Just a little though; they were only fairies of course.

Then that purple fairy approached us. Or shall I say she attacked us? She was absolutely stunning with short, curly, purple hair and a strappy dress. I didn't know what to make of her and then she blew dust all over my sisters and me. I remember trying to get away. I am not afraid of dust of course, but she pulled it from her purse, and it was purple. I assume it was not NORMAL dust because I have never known anyone to carry dust in their purse and I have never seen purple dust before. In addition, she blew it at us. Who does that? And why would anyone do that? I don't know, but none of it seemed normal.

I couldn't escape. Instead, my limbs went limp, and I fell to the floor. I remember seeing my sisters dropping to the floor also. I could not move or make a sound. I felt my eyes grow heavy and just before my eyes shut, I remember thinking, *we should have listened to our parents.*

Chapter Ten - Interrogation

Sleepily I stretch my arms and my hand caresses something smooth. Warmth surrounds me, and I smile in contentment. Where am I? I wonder drowsily. Then I remember the dust and the yellow and purple fairy, and my eyes fly open in fear.

I try to look around, but bright sunlight blinds me, and I wince in surprise. I raise my hand to shield my eyes from the light. Hearing a soft rustle, I turn towards the sound.

"Oh, are you awake, my dear," inquires a soft, motherly voice. "Tell me, how are you feeling?"

Peering through the light, I try to make out the speaker as I reply, "Um... I feel good actually. What happened?"

"I am glad that you feel well, my dear. I apologize for this, but we had to take certain measures to protect ourselves until we understand more. Now I must know why you are here?" the kind voice interrogates.

"Wait...Where are my sisters?" I ask nervously.

"All in good time, dear. First we have some questions."

"NO! I have questions. Where are my sisters?" I demand as I frantically try to stand.

"Oh, no, my dear. I am afraid we can't have any of that," the kind voice commands firmly. I feel a weight press upon me. It is gentle and firm, and it is holding me down.

"Please sit down," the voice insists.

Frustrated, I began to cry. "Why are you doing this to me?" I sob.

"Don't cry," the voice reassures. "Everything will be okay. Please have some tea and calm down."

I am shocked to observe a dainty dusty rose tea set float towards me as she is speaking. It is ornate and decorated with a silver moon and stars that appear to shimmer. It looks new, bright, and clean but very old-fashioned. It reminds me of the fence and how it was in such great shape, yet it must have been there for years. Looking closer I realize that the stars on the tea set form constellations.

"Please understand that you have frightened us," the voice admits. "We have not even glimpsed a human for many years, let alone had one here among us. How long have you been in our Realm? Why have we never noticed you before? Where were you hiding?" she questions me.

The stars on the tea set seem to glow and begin to shift. Fantastically the stars slowly move.

Rhythmically they grow bright, then dim as different shapes form and disappear on the tea set. The teacup begins to slowly dance around the teapot.

"Hiding? We weren't hiding!" I squeak as I keep my eyes on the floating tea set.

"Where did you come from?" she presses.

This cannot be happening, I think. I must be imagining this. I probably hit my head when I fell. I obviously hit my head hard. I think as I become aware of a voice answering the questions asked by the mysterious, unseen gentle voice.

"We came from the other side of the fence," I hear, and am shocked to recognize that is my voice speaking! I feel my mouth begin to move, to form words, and even as I try to stop my mouth from moving, I hear my voice replying, "We were just curious. We thought we saw something beneath the waterfall, and we wanted to know what it was."

"You came from the other side of the fence?" the voice repeats slowly. "What fence do you speak of?"

Again, I find myself responding against my will. "The fence on the other side of the waterfall and across the meadow."

"What?" she gasps. "That is impossible. No one has been able to cross since, since, since...the incident." Waving her hand, she dismisses, "Never mind that. How did you get past the guardian?"

"Guardian? I don't remember any guardian. We had no trouble crossing the fence. In fact, I felt like we were greeted."

"Impossible! This is a ridiculous story! Now please, PLEASE focus on the teapot and tell me the truth!" the voice demands.

I become aware that my eyes are searching for the tea set. I try to stop myself but cannot. I manage a small grunt as I struggle against looking at the teapot.

"Don't fight it," the voice advises reassuringly. "Surely you must be beginning to understand that nothing hurts here. There will be nothing unpleasant about this. I just need you to answer my questions."

I remember the dust in my face and falling asleep only to awaken refreshed and comfortable. Everything in this strange land has been pleasant and beautiful, I think. Even being drugged (as I assume, I was with that dust) and waking up on the ground, I feel refreshed when I should feel stiff and exhausted.

Distracted by my thoughts, I am disappointed to realize that I am again staring at the teapot. It is positively mesmerizing, and I begin relaxing against my will.

Dazed I reply, "Everything that I have told you is the truth."

"What are your intentions? Will you harm us or steal from us?" the voice demands.

"What!? Never!" I exclaim in shock. "Whatever this place is, I think it is the most beautiful land I have ever seen. I want to know everything about this fantastic place."

The mysterious voice is quiet. *I hope that is a good sign*, I think as I try to look around. I glimpse movement from the corner of my eye and find that I can turn my head now. I look away from the teapot and my gaze falls upon a plump, rosy-cheeked fairy that materializes out of thin air.

The elderly fairy has gray hair that sparkles in the light and large, calm eyes. She acts as if deep in thought as she slowly comes forward. Only her face is visible, then she shifts and the rest of herself is revealed as she appears to be removing an unseen cape. Though I cannot distinguish any fabric, the fairy acts as if she is handling something that she folds and puts in a purse that she has on her shoulder. She looks at me, and I am stunned; she looks like my Grandma Jean, my dad's mom.

How is this possible?

She wears an apron covered with real white flowers, and from her pocket she pulls a matching handkerchief.

Examining her closer, I notice some differences from my grandmother. While her face looks exactly the same as Grandma Jean, my actual grandmother has short, perfect, professional gray hair and wears very little makeup. This fairy, while her hair is short, it is messy, and her makeup is dramatic and flashy with bright red lipstick and pink eyeshadow.

Oh, my grandmother would never allow me to wear such bright makeup, let alone wear it herself. The jewelry is also different. Grandma always wore dainty pearls whereas this fairy has delicate white flowers draped all over her. Small flowers dangle from her ear lobes while huge versions of the same flower hang heavily from her wrists. A necklace of woven flowers circles her plump neck, and individual flowers are poking out of her hair.

She contemplates me seriously for a moment before announcing, "I am Salvia," and offers me her handkerchief.

"What!?" I yelp. "How can you look like my grandmother!?"

Smiling, she discloses, "Darling, I am everyone's grandma. That is my gift. Everyone sees their grandmother in me, and I know and can create some of their most treasured memories that they had with their grandmother. Open the handkerchief," she instructs me.

I am surprised to notice that I took her handkerchief and that it is in my hand. *How does she do that*, I wonder.

Opening it slowly, I am shocked to find a fresh baked, warm, chocolate chip cookie. The sweet smell makes my mouth water. I probably shouldn't eat this cookie, I think. Mother has always said to never take food from a stranger, and I have never known anyone stranger than this Salvia. My stomach growls though, and I realize that I am starving.

Oh, what do I have to lose, I think. Even though she looks innocent, she just had tea sets flying around. If she wanted to hurt me, she could, and this cookie smells amazing. Taking a small bite, it melts in my mouth and has a slight, surprising taste of mint. My eyes widen. This is MY Grandma Jean's mint cookies.

"It is impossible to lie to me," Salvia admits. "So I know that what you told me is the truth. The other fairies depend on me to unearth the truth."

Hearing a commotion, I look up as the side doors are pushed open. In marches a small group of oddly dressed fairies. They are all wearing slim fitting, silky green gowns with full length capes. The capes are stunning and are all in different colors.

One cape is a blinding yellow, another is a vicious red, then a pastel pink, purple, peach, orange, and even a brilliant blue. Their large wings are the same colors as their capes, and on their hips, they each have what appears to be a long sword with wooden handles. Matching wooden shields are on their backs nestled between their large wings.

"Where is the human? We need to get to the bottom of this now," a loud voice declares from the approaching group. "Salvia, may we please have your report?"

Upon observing me, the group stops short. The red and peach caped fairies step forward, drawing their swords. I realize that they are actually long, thin wands, not swords. *Of course they are wands*, I think. These are fairies, not gladiators.

Salvia rushes towards them, and the approaching fairies pause. I detect hushed, quick discussions. Watching them I notice the pink fairy that I had bumped into earlier coming through the door. She moves quietly and comes in slowly. As if she is trying to not draw any attention to herself. I catch her eye, and she puts her finger to her lips, signaling me to stay quiet.

Interesting, I think. Why is she here? What was her name I wonder? I think it started with a "E." Ethel? No. Emily? No. Geez, I wish I was better with names!

Looking back to the group of fairies in front of me, I interrupt softly, "Excuse me." No one seems to hear me. Raising my voice, I repeat loudly, "EXCUSE ME!"

The commotion stops, and the fairies turn towards me. "What is going on here?" I demand bravely. "Where am I, and where are my sisters? And who are you?" I ask, pointing a shaky finger towards the fairies dressed in green.

Their eyes widen, and they look at each other. After a moment's hesitation, the tallest among them steps forward. He is wearing a brilliant blue cape and has long blond hair that is neatly pulled back into a tight knot on the back of his head.

His eyes are even brighter blue than his cape, and he speaks clearly to me, "We are the Glads, and you are in the great Realm of the Fairies. You have crossed the meadow that separates our world from yours," he explains. "This should not have been possible. You and the others who came with you knew where we were and knew how to get past the Guardian. No human should know these things."

"We just found you. We didn't know…" I interrupted him.

He calmly raises his hand to silence me before proceeding, "Until we know who you are and why you came here, we must put you in the Fairy Fort for safe keeping."

"What!?" I squeak in fear.

He raises his wand and twirls it quickly in tight circles in the air while never taking his eyes off mine. I am stunned to see a blue ray of light coming from the end of his wand. As he twirls his wand, the light grows longer and curls around me. I feel it tightening around me, and I squeal in surprise as I am lifted off of the ground. I struggle to get free.

Fairy Fort! I don't like the sound of that, I think as I struggle frantically against the blue light. My arms are held tightly against me by the blue light, which feels soft, thick, and rubbery. Pushing with all my strength, I am able to move my right arm a few inches from my body. The further my arm gets from my body, the more tension I feel against my arm.

It's as if I have a giant blue rubber band around me and my arm snaps back to my side.

I look around and notice the eyes of my captor. What was his name, I wonder? Was it Glad? *What a strange name for a strong-looking warrior fairy*, I think. Glad's eyes are focused on me, and he looks very strained as if this is taking all of his energy. And… there is something more. The expression on his face…. he looks very surprised.

Why would he be surprised? I am the one being lifted into the air by magical blue light. I stop struggling as I ponder this, and I immediately began to fly through the air. It is so fast that my head snaps back and the speed takes my breath away as I rush out of the room. Before he is out of view, I catch one more look at Glad and am surprised to recognize relief upon his face.

Chapter Eleven – Fairy Fort

As I whiz by the tunnels, the air grows cooler and damper. Everything that I pass is a blur of color, and I travel so quickly that by the time I reach my destination, I am completely disoriented. Abruptly I stop, and the blue light loosens around me, allowing me to gently slip to the floor.

I shut my eyes and try to make my head stop spinning. After taking a few deep breaths, I slowly open my eyes and look around.

I am in a darkened room with no windows. *This must be the Fairy Fort*, I think. It must be some kind of fairy jail, but I don't see any bars. This room is almost empty, except for a fairy-sized wrought iron table with a matching chair in one corner. In the other corner, there is a human-sized bed. The only decoration is a large red vase bursting with flowers in the corner. I put my hands on the stone floor and slowly push myself up into a standing position. I brace myself against the wall and am surprised that all of the walls, floor, ceiling, and even the door are made of stone. I walk shakily to the bed and gratefully fall into it. I am thankful that this glorious bed is large enough for me. The fabric that I am on is the same shade of red as the vase and is soft and thick. Like the softest velvet I have ever felt.

As I lay there, I can smell the flowers, and the scent reminds me of my mother.

Oh, Dad, I think, *I wish I had never disobeyed you and had never come here.* My eyes tear up, and I quietly begin to cry. What will happen to me, and where in the world are my sisters, I wonder. My eyes are heavy, and I feel exhausted after everything that has happened. Reluctantly I give in and fall into a deep sleep.

Chapter Twelve – Bubble Who

My eyes fly open, and I look around with a start. I remember being placed in this room and being so worn out that I fell asleep. What woke me up? Then I hear it again......baa....... baa followed by a giggle. Turning quickly to face the unfamiliar sounds, I am greeted with a strange sight. A little goat is next to the bed. Its eyes are staring directly into my eyes, and it is so close that it is almost touching me.

I jerk away from the animal as it leans closer to try to nibble on my shirt. It is white with big brown splotches of color scattered across its body. It is no larger than a puppy and it has two little horns and a long beard. Noticing me studying it, the goat baas at me again and cocks its head to one side. She then walks over to the flower vase in the corner, knocks it over and begins sniffing and rooting around in the flowers.

Standing upright quickly, the goat looks back at me as it chews loudly on something that it found. I squint in the dim light and recognize that it has flowers in its mouth. With every chew, the flowers flip and flop, and they look like they should fall right out of the goat's little mouth. The goat's beard sways crazily with every bite, and the goat is chewing furiously fast as if the flowers might get away. It is so comical that I laugh out loud.

Hearing my laugh, the goat baas at me while somehow losing only some of the flowers in its mouth. It flicks its tail back and forth and looks even more like a puppy wagging its tail than before. Then the goat sashays over to me and pushes its head against my hand, frantically chewing the entire time. Forgetting everything I affectionately pet the strange little creature, and its tail wags in friendliness.

"That is enough now, Bubble Gum, come here, girl!" a friendly voice calls from the shadows. I sit up in surprise, and the goat, Bubble Gum I assume, flicks its tail and struts towards the voice, leaving a trail of chewed flowers behind her.

"Who…who is there?" I ask nervously.

The pink fairy that bumped into me and landed in my hand earlier comes into the light. She pauses in hesitation, then addresses me, "It is me, Easter, and this is my loyal Bubble Gum." She motions towards the goat that is busy foraging through the vase looking for more flowers.

At a loss of how to respond, I question, "Why do you call her Bubble Gum?"

Smiling brightly at me, Easter answers, "Because of this." Glowing with happiness, Easter turns towards the goat and digs into the pocket of her pink dress. Pulling something out, she holds her hand towards the goat and calls out, "Oh, Bubble Gum! I have a treat for you!"

Bubble Gum snaps her head out of the vase, and I laugh to see that she has flowers clinging to her ears and stuck in between her horns. She spits her half-chewed flowers on the ground as she excitedly dashes towards Easter, flowers falling off of her in every direction as she hurries over.

Reaching Easter, she stands on her hind legs and clumsily jumps towards Easter's hand. Easter flies above her and opens her hand to drop a small pink object to the goat. Bubble Gum excitedly catches the object in her mouth, and dropping onto all fours, chews energetically.

"Watch," commands Easter, looking affectionately towards the little goat.

Bubble Gum stops chewing and begins to spit and sputter as something pink comes out of her mouth.

"She's choking!" I cry out in alarm as I jump off the bed.

Then before I can move any closer to rescue the poor animal, the pink thing in her mouth grows larger, and Bubble Gum's head tilts back as the goat slowly lifts off of the ground. Pulled up into the air by the enormous, pink…bubble that is coming out of her mouth. My jaw drops in surprise as Easter giggles.

"It is enchanted bubble gum," Easter squeals in delight. "It is her FAVOR-ITE. So, her name is Bubble Gum."

The bubble pops, and Bubble Gum falls to the ground baaing happily. Standing quickly and swishing her tail in excitement, she immediately begins to chew then blow another bubble.

Despite how strange everything is, I laugh. "That is amazing," I remark truthfully as I watch the little goat's new bubble pop and she falls to the floor. She promptly begins to chew on her piece of gum trying to make another bubble.

"Goats are very playful," Easter comments while swooping down to give Bubble Gum a scratch on her forehead. "They are intelligent, kind, and silly. You humans have dogs, we fairies prefer goats."

"I have never had a goat," I tell her. "Do they only eat flowers?"

Laughing, Easter replies, "Of course not, that would be silly!"

"Oh," I utter, feeling a little embarrassed.

"They eat almost EVERYTHING," Easter estimates in delight, "and they LOVE trying new things!"

I smile as I look back at the goat that is floating around the room, happily hanging from a giant pink bubble. Then I look towards Easter, and clearing my throat, I timidly ask, "Why am I here, in this room?"

Chapter Thirteen - Tell Me

Looking at me, Easter replies, "This is our safest place. Deep within the falls, where no one can see or hear us. Magic cannot penetrate the rock, and magical beings cannot escape the Fairy Fort."

"I am not magical," I deny quickly.

"So, you claim," Easter acknowledges. "But we haven't seen humans for many years. As far as we knew, humans were no longer able to cross into our realm, and we were not able to cross into theirs. We put you here while we discussed what we should do."

"What you should do? About what?"

"Not what. Whom. We had to decide what should be done about you."

"Oh," I said, feeling nervous. "And...and what did you decide?"

Easter smiles at me reassuringly and relents, "We decided that you meant us no harm when you came here."

"Well, that's good," I comment quietly. "I really would never hurt anyone."

"I believe you. And Salvia saw nothing dangerous about you at all. But I do need to understand how you were able to come here," Easter asserts, looking at me seriously. "Before...the incident, we could cross into the human realm, but now our realm is shielded, so that humans cannot detect us or come here. Humans walk right by the fence and never notice it," she explains. "From time to time, a fairy would allow a human to observe the fence. It has happened before where a fairy invited a human to come into our world, but it has always been discouraged; we like our privacy," Easter confesses smiling. "Since the incident though, even if a fairy wished for it, no human could locate the fence. This is why we are so troubled by you crossing."

"What is this incident everyone keeps talking about?" I ask confused.

"We call it that because it is too terrible to call it by name," Easter replies somberly. Then taking a deep breath, she resumes, "Years ago a fairy began to experiment with the dark art of using her powers for evil. She believed that we fairies shouldn't 'hide' in the Fairy Realm but claim our rightful place as leaders, or Gods, over all the other creatures. Initially everyone in the realm rejected these ideas. Eventually though she was able to convince a few fairies and other creatures to join her cause, and they began to plan to take over the realms. No one knew the actual name of this dark fairy, so she was referred to as Banshee. When the Fairy leaders realized what Banshee was up to, they ordered her arrest. But before she could be located, she escaped into the human world. When she departed the Fairy Realm, she sealed the fence, so that we could not follow her. Since then, we have not been able to cross...."

"What? A fairy is in our world? That can't be. I have never noticed a fairy before now," I object.

Smiling, Easter replies, "Fairies have many powers and gifts. If a fairy does not want to be discovered, she won't be. The greatest protection that we have from being found is your disbelief."

"What do you mean?"

"You have heard about fairies, haven't you?"

"Of course I have."

"Then why were you surprised to find us?" Easter asks me, raising a questioning eyebrow at me.

"Well...I just have never seen any fairies before."

"Uh, uh. Have you ever learned about leprechauns? Don't you even have cereal with a picture of a leprechaun on it in the Human Realm?"

"Sure, everyone knows about leprechauns and how they hide their gold at the end of rainbows. But that is just a story."

"Just like how fairies were just a story before yesterday. The Leprechauns are my distant cousins, and they are terrible tricksters. Always up to something. They play pranks on everyone. But they do make the BEST shoes, don't you think?" Easter asks as she looks down and points towards her dainty feet, which have neon pink ballet-looking slippers on them.

"Yes, they are pretty, but…What!? They exist AND they are your cousins!?"

"Of course they exist. Leprechauns are all over in the Human Realm. But you are wrong about their gold. They are just poor shoemakers playing a joke on everyone. Oh, how they love to watch humans chase the rainbows, trying to find the gold. It gives them a good laugh. They use their magic to hide the end of the rainbow, so that no matter how close you are, it always seems to move away."

"But if no fairies can cross the meadow, how can leprechauns?"

"They just love to play tricks on humans. Most of them live in your realm because they love it so much. Hiding your keys or moving your shoes. And socks! They just love socks! They snatch socks out of dryers and collect them. They all have piles and piles of socks that they play in like it is snow. How they giggle when humans have missing socks. They should be ashamed of themselves for all of the fights they have started between humans when they are trying to locate a pair of matching socks."

"So leprechauns live in my world?"

"Most of them do," Easter replies. "They are different than fairies in that they travel using rainbows. Whenever you notice a rainbow, you know leprechauns are traveling from one realm to another."

"Are you suggesting that leprechauns make rainbows!?" I demand.

"What do you need in order to see a rainbow?" Easter asks me patiently.

"Well…rain and… sunlight."

"There's your answer, Ana. Rain SHOULD come out of the clouds. And if there are clouds out, it should not be sunny. Oh, those leprechauns love to make it rain during a sunny day. They laugh until their toes tickle to watch humans caught in a rainstorm while they are painting or at the beach or playing a game in the nice sunny weather."

"Whoa," I interrupt. "I remember that happening to me not that long ago. It was a beautiful sunny day, and we were watching Becca play in a soccer game. It was a championship game, and she is the team captain. She is the best soccer player on her team," I pronounce proudly. "Anyway, there wasn't a cloud in the sky, and it began to rain on us. It was a real downpour actually. Everyone got soaked!"

"And did you spy a rainbow?"

Frowning, I think, "I remember running to our car, holding my hands over my head. Tripping over my own feet and stumbling into the puddles as I tried to get out of the rain. I looked up when I heard Lizzie yell at me to watch out for another puddle, and behind her I saw......" My mouth falls open in surprise. "Yes, I do remember seeing a rainbow."

Giggling, Easter agrees, "Yep, that was definitely my cousins, the Leprechauns. They love to cause trouble. They are a happy group though and they always have great stories."

Shaking my head in wonder, I start to smile. "Well, I can understand how everyone must have looked pretty funny running around in the rain. Mrs. Beazley was absolutely furious because she had just had her hair done for a party that night. She was so mad that she went from shrieking to crying. But that is okay, I suppose, because she was yelling before it started raining, too. She was screaming at her daughter who was playing on the soccer field," I continued. "It isn't that her daughter is bad at soccer, she just isn't as good as my sister. But no one else is as good as Becca. I am glad that Mrs. Beazley's hair got ruined," I declare. "She is a mean woman. Good for the leprechauns. Please thank them for that."

Smiling, Easter replies, "Oh, I will."

Looking at Easter, I admit slowly, "I am wondering about one thing though."

Chapter Fourteen - The Jays

"Just one thing? I have many, many, many questions for you," Easter laughs.

"Well, yes I have MANY questions. But Salvia had mentioned someone called Guardian who she said should have stopped us. Who is that?"

"The Guardian is a strong, magnificent horse who lives in the meadow. He has sworn to protect us from intruders and enemies."

"The horse!?" I squeak in surprise.

"Of course, couldn't you tell?" Easter asks me while tossing her long pink hair over one shoulder. "His keen eyesight and amazing senses allow him to notice things before they happen, and he can smell someone's aura and knows from where they have come and what their intentions are."

"See things before they happen?" I repeat. "He looked surprised by the Blue Jays when they attacked."

Frowning, Easter pries, "How do you know about the Jays?"

"We saw them before we crossed. It looked like they were attacking."

"And you still crossed the fence?" Easter asks in shock. "Weren't you scared?"

"Scared of Blue Jays?" I reply in disbelief. "Why would we be scared of birds?"

"Those aren't normal Blue Jays," Easter remarks quietly. "They are enchanted by the evil force that remains after the incident. They keep watch on our entrance and try to get behind the waterfall, trying to enter our Fairy Realm just as you did."

"Their screams are so hideous that it knocks us out of the air. Even if we aren't injured from the fall, we are helplessly stunned on the ground, unable to walk, let alone fly. Awake but unable to call for help. It is terrifying," Easter admits, shivering in fear.

"What were the other birds that looked like they were fighting the Jays?" I ask.

"The Gales? Oh, yes, Nightingales is the name you know them by I believe. They are brave knights who are loyal to the Fairies. We have been friends since the beginning of time. When the first Fairies met the Gales, we saw the goodness in them and gave the Nightingales the enchantment of song. The Gales were able to sing sweet songs that are as sweet as they are. We have been best friends ever since. The Jays hate the Gales."

Suddenly there is a loud POP followed by a bleat and a crash. Twirling we discover Bubble Gum lying on her back on top of the bed, covered with the stinky, pink gum. Her legs thrash as she tries to stand, but the gum is everywhere, stuck in her fur and on her horns. Tying her legs together and sticking her to the blankets. Laughing in spite of her obvious distress, I rush towards the panicked goat.

"Hush, girl, it is okay. We will get you out of this…somehow," I utter doubtfully as I pull at the gum, which remains unchanged by my efforts.

"Step away and I will help her," Easter directs. Looking up I observe her pull a delicate pink wand from between her wings. Quickly I jump away from Bubble Gum, remembering the powerful blue light that came out of the last wand I saw. I gulp in fear and have the strong urge to close my eyes. Forcing my eyes to remain open, my heart thumps wildly in my chest as I watch in amazement.

Twirling her wand gracefully through the air in a light, sweeping motion, a pink, sparkly dust dances out of Easter's wand and circles Bubble Gum. The goat bleats wildly and thrashes her legs as the dust settles upon her. As Bubble Gum is covered with dust, she relaxes, and her eyes shut halfway as though she is being petted by the mysterious, glittery cloud.

The gum covering her begins to disappear, and she is gently lifted and stood on her feet. The room clears, and Bubble Gum stands proudly in the middle of the room, happy, clean and not sticky anymore. Even the bed, which was covered with goat and gum a minute ago, is now made, and the bedding looks as if it had just been washed.

My mouth drops open in surprise, and I exclaim, "Holy cow, how did you do that?"

Smiling, Easter asks me, "Would you like to understand?"

Chapter Fifteen - Gifts

Forgetting everything else, I quickly respond, "Yes! Yes, I want to know everything about this place."

"Then follow me," Easter replies as she moves towards the door, leaving a trail of pink glitter behind her. She silently hovers just above the ground as her delicate wings flutter so quickly that all I make out is a faint blur of glitter. She swipes her hand from left to right and the door opens.

"Aren't you afraid that I will escape?" I ask her. I immediately regret voicing anything and groan in frustration. Why am I so dumb? Here I go, saying the wrong thing and ruining my chance to explore this amazing place and possibly ruining my chance to escape.

Raising one delicate eyebrow, Easter questions me, "Would you rather stay in the Fort?"

"No. No, definitely not," I insist quickly.

"Very well, come along. You, too, Bubble Gum."

Raising her head, Bubble Gum swishes her tail in excitement and sashays after Easter. I follow Bubble Gum. Exiting the room, I again see stained glass everywhere.

Beautiful, detailed, and intricate pictures in breath-taking colors cover the walls. Light flows freely from them and fills the room.

Bubble Gum stops to sniff one of the stained-glass windows, and I realize the picture is of a goat. A goat that looks a lot like Bubble Gum except that she has the same fairy wings as Easter and is hovering above a field of flowers. The goat in the picture has a mouthful of flowers, which are falling from her mouth as she tries to eat too many at once. A dreamy expression is on the goat's face as she gazes lovingly at the flowers below.

I jump as Bubble Gum sighs happily before turning away from the stained glass and continuing to follow Easter.

"Did Bubble Gum just sigh?" I ask loudly. "Goats don't sigh."

"Goats sigh here," Easter answers. "That picture is one of Bubble Gum's dreams. It is one of her favorites, and she always loves to admire it when we pass."

"Goats dream?" I repeat stupidly.

Laughing, Easter implores me, "Why wouldn't they?"

"Okay. Well even if goats dream, how can a picture of her dream be in that stained glass we just walked by?"

"I know what all creatures dream," Easter replies. "It is my gift. Let me ask you, Ana, what does Easter mean to you? It is a holiday for humans, isn't it?"

"Easter is…rabbits I suppose." Then blushing I continue, "I mean that is the first thing that I think of is the Easter Bunny. Then chicks and eggs and… . flowers……springtime," I trail off lamely.

Smiling kindly, Easter acknowledges, "Easter celebrates new life and hope. It is a time when babies are born and the flowers bloom. When snow melts and the grass begins to turn green, flowers bud and apple trees blossom. All plants and creatures are filled with happiness and hope for the new spring. I know what all creatures dream of and hope for and I am able to make it possible," she confesses. "That is why the holiday is named after me. The only reason why Bubble Gum doesn't have actual wings is because goats are terribly careless, and she would injure herself constantly. Plus, she thinks the gum is fun."

"Wait, wait a minute. The holiday is named after YOU!? Surely you mean that you are named after the holiday. People have been celebrating Easter for over a thousand years. You can't be any older than then, then…twenty-three maybe?" I speculate doubtfully.

At this Easter throws her head back and laughs. It is a splendid sound. Sweet and soft and musical.

Wiping tears from her eyes, Easter observes "Oh, you are so young and so innocent. We Fairies are timeless. I am much, much older than that. You could say that I am as old as the stars."

As we talked, I followed Easter until she stopped in front of a large, thick curtain made of amazing flowers that glowed and swayed in front of us.

"Are you ready to discover it? Are you ready to check out the Realm?" Easter asks me excitedly.

Still trying to understand that fairies are as old as the stars I stammer, "What? Sorry…"

"The Realm," Easter repeats. "Are you ready to explore the Fairy Realm?'

"I thought we were already in the Realm," I ask confused.

"Oh, no. Everything that you have seen thus far has been part of the barrier between our worlds. This. This is our Realm," Easter pronounces as the curtain grandly parts.

Chapter Sixteen - The Realm

L ight and warmth overcomes me as I step slowly through the curtain and
gasp in delight.

Covering my mouth with my hands, I try to open my eyes wider than
they have ever been before, trying desperately to take in everything. The
fragrance of flowers greets me, and the first thing I observe is the wondrous
sky. The moon is centered directly above us and is larger and brighter than
I have ever seen it before. From that middle point, the sky is divided into
five distinct sections.

One part has the most breathtaking sunrise I have ever witnessed, bright
and vibrant, fresh and bright. The next has the sun shining brightly and just a
few clouds in the blue sky.

Then the nighttime sky, with more stars than I have ever detected before, and they look bigger and brighter and closer than I ever imagined they
could be. A cloudy, gray section with rain coming down steadily is next to
that, then finally a section showing the most calming, serene sunset that I
have ever witnessed.

Lowering my eyes, I realize that we are on the side of a hill, and before us
is a peaceful country scene with small cottages scattered throughout fields with
rolling hills. A little dirt road winds between the trees and to the cottages.

Glorious waterfalls cascade down the rocky hillsides and calm into sweet
streams that zig zag here and there in the valley and out of sight. Birds sing in

the air, and there are flowers and goats everywhere. I hear laughter and music coming from cottages, which are made of stone and have roofs covered with grass and flowers.

I giggle to spy little goats happily jumping up the sides of the hills and bouncing onto the roofs of the cottages. They are chewing on anything that they come to. One is tasting a grass covered roof, another is tangled up in a bush eating berries, and another is eating flowers from the flower boxes under a window. Then I notice that the goats here are smaller than the tiny fairies.

I turn towards Easter and am surprised to realize that I am looking her in the eye. Looking down at myself, I see that I look the same, but now Easter and I are the same size.

"How are you so big all of a sudden?" I ask her.

Easter laughs, "I have not changed," she disagrees. "You have. You would have been too big for our Realm, so I made you fairy sized. The goats also shrink to our size."

I glance at Bubble Gum, who is leaning against Easter and who now comes up to Easter's waist.

"Will I go back to my normal size?" I squeak nervously.

"Oh, yes, once you leave the Fairy Realm, you will go back to your normal size," she assures me. Then Easter claps her hands in excitement and reaches out to reassuringly take my hand. "Come with me," she invites with her eyes twinkling in happiness.

Chapter Seventeen - Importance of Flowers

As we begin down the rocky path, I notice a small fairy. He is dressed in a simple white outfit and has a white baby goat snuggled in his arms. The baby goat is absently chewing on what appears to be a dandelion as the small fairy floats up the path.

Noticing us the boy bows at Easter and greets her, "Good day, My Grace."

"And what a good day it is, isn't it, Little Spider?" Easter replies. "How is your lovely mother, Virginia?"

Blushing happily the small fairy answers, "She is well, My Grace. She is just over there tending to our garden," he says, pointing down the hillside.

Looking around the boy, I glimpse a lovely fairy in a simple purple dress weeding a garden.

As we continue our stroll down the path, I turn towards Easter and ask, "What did he mean by Your Grace?"

"Oh, it's nothing," she replies, waving her perfect delicate hand dismissively. "My full name is Easter Lily of the Fairy Lilys. The Lily family are the leaders of the Fairy Realm. My mother's name is Royal Lily, and she is our Supreme Ruler."

"What does that mean? Are you a princess?" I grill her, my eyes growing even wider.

"Yes, I suppose you may call me a princess. Though we don't follow the human rules of a monarchy. Instead, our entire family is considered...a leader in the community. One of us is elected to be the Supreme Ruler for a term not to exceed 100 years. Then we will hold elections for the new Supreme."

"Lilly...Royal..Salvia...Aren't Royal Lily and Salvia both flowers?" I ask Easter.

"Of course, they are, silly. Right along with the common Small Leaf SPI-DERwort and the larger VIRGINIA Spiderwort. Both of whom you just met."

"What?" I gasp. "Both of those fairies that we just met are named after flowers. Spiderworts?"

"Humans have a lot to learn," Easter remarks smiling. "Or maybe it is just that you are so, so young. Back to your questions, yes and yes. Those were the Spiderworts that you just met, and Salvia is a beautiful white and pink flower. Salvia has been used for generations to cause hallucinations and visions. They also cause humans to feel detached from themselves for a time."

"That is exactly how I felt when Salvia was questioning me," I comment thoughtfully. "I felt like my body was acting by itself and I couldn't stop myself from doing what she instructed me to do."

"Precisely. Salvia made the flower and the flower is named after her. Have you ever heard of the Passion Flower?" Easter quizzes me grinning.

Frowning, I think hard. "Yes, I remember that they are supposed to be extraordinarily beautiful. With a vibrant yellow middle that blends into purple petals with purple...." I trail off as my mind races.

"Yes, with purple 'tassels' that come from the middle of the flower and dangle over the petals. "

"That sounds like the fairy who drugged me with the dust!" I cry out.

"Exactly," agrees Easter. "That was Passion. Passion Flowers relieve anxiety and cause sleepiness. She used her flower power to put you to sleep. Each fairy is able to intensify and focus the abilities of their flower."

"Are any of you dangerous?" I ask, remembering the strength of Passion's dust. "What about that Blue Fairy named Glad who put me in the Fort? He was...scary," I admit as I shiver at the memory.

"Oh, that was Gladiolus," disclosures Easter smiling. "We call them Glads for short; they think it sounds tougher than Gladiolus," Easter whispers to me smiling. "The Gladiolus family has served the Lily family loyally for generations. In your world, they earned the nickname of the Sword Lily due to their height and strength. They are our protectors."

Chapter Eighteen - Magic

We are interrupted by Bubble Gum, who races up to Easter. Baaing, she dances around Easter jumping on her hind legs in excitement. Giggling at her eagerness, Easter reaches into her pocket and pulls out something for the small goat.

Quickly Bubble Gum licks up the treat in Easter's hand and dashes away from us. Twitching her tail and chewing furiously, Bubble Gum begins running towards the edge of the cliff that we are standing upon.

Gasping, I began to run towards her in alarm. "Bubble Gum!" I scream out. "STOP! Oh, no...." I cry out as Bubble Gum runs over the edge and disappears out of sight.

I stop at the edge of the cliff and look down nervously.

My mouth drops open in surprise to observe the small goat hovering just below me. Her head is thrown back and she has a gigantic pink bubble coming from her mouth. Her tail is wagging back and forth in excitement as she floats away from us and slowly descends towards some apple trees. Rather than go around the trees, she heads straight into them. There is a loud POP when her bubble hits the tree limbs and bursts that makes me wince and I shut my eyes.

Opening my eyes, I laugh to see Bubble Gum in the branches of the apple tree, covered in pink goo. Rather than be alarmed, she stretches out her neck and bites the nearest apple. Apple chunks fall from her mouth in all directions while she chews as fast as she can. Looking at us, she baas happily, then proceeds to suck another apple into her mouth.

Giggling over the silly goat, I ask Easter, "How will she ever get down? That gum is everywhere."

"I will help her in a few minutes," Easter replies. "This is her favorite way to eat apples. She doesn't like the ones that have already fallen off of the tree and are on the ground. It is much more fun and easier to just be in the tree with the apples."

Feeling dizzy I put my hand to my head and murmur, "My mind is spinning with all of this new information. I think I need to sit down for a minute."

Looking concerned Easter pulls her pink wand from between her wings and points it just behind me. My eyes follow the pink glitter that dances from her wand, in the air and gathers behind me. It gets so thick that I cannot see through it, and I step away in fear. *What is she doing now*, I wonder.

Then almost as quickly as it had appeared, the dust cloud thins, and I can make out an object that wasn't there before. It becomes clearer, and my mouth drops open in surprise to discover a beautiful pink wicker patio set. The love seat and chair are covered with delicate flowers, and I reach out to gently caress the soft petals.

"Oh, I almost forgot," Easter apologizes, and with a snap of her wand, a delicate crystal pitcher and glasses materialize on the tabletop, along with a huge pink lily in a matching vase as a centerpiece. The pitcher is clear and empty. *Hmm, I wonder what fairies drink*, I think as I stare appreciatively at the beautiful scene.

"Sit down, Ana," Easter commands me and I sit immediately. Cautiously I settle into the petal-covered wicker chair and am relieved to find that it is very comfortable, and I begin to relax.

"Would you like some tea, Ana?" Easter asks me. "It is my favorite, Rose Tea."

I nod smiling, "Yes, please. I LOVE tea." I lean towards the table, excited to try fairy tea.

Easter waves her wand over the pitcher, and it fills up with a pretty pink-colored liquid.

Easter twirls her wand next to her, and Bubble Gum appears in a pink cloud. She is clean and gum free but still has apples in her mouth. Unfazed by her change in surroundings, she bends down and begins to chew on some daisies, even though she still has apples in her mouth.

"Would you like any honey with your tea?" Easter asks me kindly.

"Uh, yes please," I reply clumsily.

I hear a slight buzzing sound and am surprised to see bees flying towards us.

Alarmed I jumped up from my seat, ready to run away from the approaching bees.

"Oh, I forgot that humans are afraid of bees," Easter exclaims. "Please sit down; there is nothing to be afraid of Ana. The bees are our friends and we work together. Fairies grow flowers, which the bees pollinate. Then the bees make honey, which we use to sweeten our tea. Watch," Easter instructs me.

Sitting down carefully, I watch with wide eyes as the bees approach. They are in an organized line, and it appears that they are each carrying something. As each one passes over my glass, they pause briefly.

Easter holds out her hand to one of them, and it carefully lands in the palm of her hand. She extends her hand towards me, and I look closer at the bee. My mouth drops open in surprise to discover that the little bee is carrying a small pitcher full of an amber-colored liquid.

Looking into my glass, I notice that there is now a small amount of amber-colored liquid in my glass and that more bees are pouring their pitchers into my glass.

"Amazing," I say.

"Yes, bees are truly amazing," Easter agrees warmly.

Bubble Gum had been happily chewing on daisies when she suddenly spits the flowers from her mouth and baas loudly. She is shaking her head frantically from side to side and running in circles. I watch bees gather over the flowers that she spat on the ground and realize what must have happened.

"Oh, Bubble Gum!" Easter exclaims in concern. "Did you get stung? Come here, let me help you."

Bubble Gum slowly walks towards Easter, making a wide arc around the bees and still shaking her head. Looking suspiciously at the bees, Bubble Gum baas loudly at them and tries to stomp on some bees that are near her on the ground.

"Stop that, Bubble Gum. It was an accident. Let me take a look at you. Where does it hurt?" Easter asks the small goat.

Bubble Gum gives the bees another dirty look and lifts her chin so that Easter can inspect a large welt that is forming just below her lower lip.

"There, there, Bubble Gum," Easter reassures. She twirls her wand over the sting, and I can see Bubble Gum relax as the pain eases.

"All better?" she questions the small goat while scratching her on the head.

Bubble Gum baas happily in reply and wags her tail.

A bee flies by her head, and she angrily snaps at it and successfully catches the bee in her mouth.

Easter and I exchange worried looks. "Are you okay, Bubble Gum?" I ask as I lean towards her. She wags her tail happily, and I can detect a faint buzzing from inside her mouth. "She looks pretty pleased with herself to have caught one of those bees," I observe in concern. "Won't it sting her though?" I ask Easter.

"Normally yes," Easter replies. "I will try to…"

I never got to hear what Easter was going to do because suddenly Bubble Gum stopped wagging her tail and froze. A look of panic overcomes the goat, and her eyes widen in surprise. Her mouth opens, and Bubble Gum emits a loud, anguished scream. One tiny little bee quickly flies from her mouth in escape.

With a look of shocked terror on her face, Bubble Gum jumps straight up into the air and goes bananas. She throws her head from side to side, spitting, screaming, baaing and jumping all over the wicker set. The chairs and the table crash loudly to the ground. I attempt to catch the pitcher before it hits the ground, but I only succeed in knocking the vase off the table. I watch helplessly as it follows the pitcher, and they both crash on the hard ground.

It is absolute chaos. I am surrounded by broken furniture, trampled flowers, and shattered crystal while Bubble Gum continues to jump and scream wildly. I begin to laugh, even though I know I shouldn't. *What did she expect*, I think. Giggling I cover my mouth with my hand just as Bubble Gum crashes into me and we are both knocked down. She puts her wet nose against my dry one, and in her terror, she screams into my face, spraying my face with goat wetness.

"Ugh, Bubble Gum! Gross! Help, help me, help us, Easter!" I sputter as I struggle to get out from under the squirming goat. Hearing laughter I look up, and sure enough, Easter is laughing. She is laughing harder than I was a moment ago. Holding her sides, Easter is laughing so hard that she is crying.

"You…two…look…look…horrible!" Easter declares in between fits of laughter.

At this Bubble Gum stops struggling and looks up at Easter. With a snort, she stands, puts her tail straight up into the air, lifts her head, and struts away from Easter. Easter reaches down to me and helps me to stand. I began to giggle as we walk towards Bubble Gum.

"I am sorry, girl," Easter apologizes to her. "I know it hurts, but if you bite a bee, you will get stung," she says, smiling. "Let me fix it."

Looking insulted Bubble Gum slowly turns towards Easter and opens her mouth, allowing Easter to look at the bee sting on her tongue. Easter twirls her wand over the goat's mouth, and pink dust slowly falls unto the little goat.

"Now are you feeling better?" Easter asks Bubble Gum. "Or shall I call a Peppermint to come and take a look at you?"

Bubble Gum snaps her mouth shut and turns away from Easter. She lifts her tail and stalks away angrily, clearly still annoyed that we laughed during her time of need.

Standing shakily I wipe…wetness from my face and confess, "I never knew goats could scream. It is a horrible noise! Is she alright?"

"She will be just fine," Easter replies as she waves her wand over the scattered ruins of our wicker patio set. The chairs and table right themselves, and the broken crystal rises from the ground. I am stunned to watch the pieces come together, and in a flash, everything is repaired and as it was before the bee stung Bubble Gum.

Bending to inspect the leg of the chair, which had been broken off a moment ago, "Amazing," I comment as I examine the chair. "It is sturdy and looks as if it was never broken. I ask, "Is a Peppermint a fairy, too?"

"Yes, and they can help a person feel better," Easter replies.

"You have been nothing but good to me, and this is all so wonderful. But it is all so much to take in. Before yesterday I never even believed in fairies."

Throwing her hands up in the air, Easter exclaims, "Oh, HUMANS! You lose faith so easily!"

"I am sorry," I say. "I never meant to offend you. I am surrounded by fairies and magic wands and glittery dust and all of these names! I wish I knew more about flowers. Then maybe I would better understand how many fairies there are and know what everyone's powers are. Lizzie would be much better at...." Then I stop entirely. Lizzie. Becca. I hadn't even thought of them. *Where are they*, I wonder. I frown and try to keep the panic from my voice as I ask quietly, "Where are my sisters?"

Suddenly looking serious, Easter replies, "Your sisters are safe, Ana. As much as I enjoy you, you and your sisters were able to come into our Fairy Realm when we believed that no human could. You got past our guardian, which should have been impossible. Then when Glad put you in the Fort, you put up such a strong fight that it took all of his strength to get you there. He is still being cared for by a Peppermint, recovering. It shouldn't have been any trouble at all for him to have gotten a human into the Fort." Leaning forward Easter asks, "Who are you, Ana?"

Chapter Nineteen - Who am I

"I...I....I am no one," I finally respond.

Easter arches a delicate brow and implores, "Tell me about yourself then...Please," she adds softly when I hesitate.

My mind feels thick and sluggish. *What would she possibly want to know about me*, I think.

"Are you a witch?" Easter asks me.

I shake my head in disbelief. "No," I reply in surprise. "I am just a girl. I have two sisters and I play tennis and I like to sing. I have two parents and... and...I am normal. I like to read and paint and I like tea..." I trail off, not knowing what else to disclose. Looking at the ground, I utter quietly, "I probably should have listened to my parents who told me not to go back to the fence."

"Wait," Easter interrupts me. "What was that last part? Your parents told you to not go back to the fence?"

"Yes," I admit slowly. "My sisters and I found the fence one day while we were walking, and when we told our parents about it, they seemed to know about the fence, and they went crazy! Mom even cried, and she never cries. Then Dad forbade us from ever going back to the fence," I confess. "They knew nothing good would come from the fence and the meadow, but they wouldn't explain, and we didn't listen to them!"

"Why?" Easter asks me carefully. "Why did you not listen to your parents?"

Looking down at my hands, I take a deep breath and answer, "Because I couldn't forget the meadow. It was all so lovely. The most beautiful place I had ever seen. I wanted to know more about it. I wanted to know everything about it. But it was more than that...it felt good to be at the fence and near the meadow. It felt safe and warm."

I paused, not wanting to say more. But there was more. This new, amazing land felt good. I felt good. Better than I had ever felt before actually. I didn't know how to describe it to Easter, but it felt like I belonged here.

Deep in thought and not appearing to notice that I had paused, Easter muses, "The Fairy Realm is safe and good, so I imagine that a human would feel that way when near it. But why did your parents act the way that they did? How could they have known anything about the fence?"

"I don't know," I responded. "They refused to talk about it."

"Had they ever mentioned the Fairy Realm before?"

"No," I answer quickly. "As far as I know, they don't even believe in fairies or magic."

"What a pity," Easter sympathizes. "I couldn't imagine a life without magic," she states with a look of sadness on her face.

"Well...I didn't believe in fairies before I met you," I admit slowly.

Waving her hand dismissively, Easter continues, "There is so much more to magic than fairies. Magic is when you meet your new best friend or when you, against all odds, make the winning goal for your team. Magic is that excitement and warmth you feel at Christmas when you know that Santa is coming. It is the joy that you feel Easter morning when you find that first Easter egg."

"I guess I don't know about all of that. We don't celebrate holidays," I confess quietly. "Mother believes they are a waste of time."

Easter's mouth falls open, then turning away from me sharply, she flies straight up into the air. A stream of pink glitter trails behind her. Zipping swiftly through the air above me, I hear her screaming out, "AH! AH!" Again and again, she screams angrily.

Not knowing what to do, I sit and wait. Slowly Easter comes closer and closer until she is pacing in the air just above me.

"Horrible. That is just horrible," Easter declares sharply. "You don't celebrate any holidays? Please tell me you celebrate Easter at least! That IS the best holiday, you know. "

Blushing, I reply, "No, I am sorry; we don't even celebrate Easter."

Easter's face falls, and she grabs me quickly in a big hug. Wrapping her delicate arms around my neck, she begins to sob loudly, "That is just the... the...the most horrible, saddest thing I have ever heard! I am so, so sorry, Ana! I am glad that you found us!"

"Really, it is okay," I croak. "You are choking me!"

"Oh, I am so sorry," Easter apologizes, loosening her grip around my neck immediately. But she resumes questioning me, "You don't decorate Easter eggs or Christmas trees? Do you make special gifts for Valentine's Day or have pumpkin pie on Thanksgiving?"

I shake my head as Easter carries on, "Don't you get gold coins on St. Patrick's Day or have charms for good luck?"

"Well...I wasn't allowed any charms, but my mother always has a moon charm," I volunteer, hoping to calm her down.

"Really?" Easter asks me in surprise. "Of all the things to have, she has a moon charm?"

"Yes," I admit. "She always has it in her pocket or around her neck. We were never allowed to touch it. But one time I snuck a look at it while she was sleeping," I confess sheepishly. "I snuck into her room while she was sleeping and very carefully took it out of her jewelry box. It just looked so interesting that I wanted to see it better."

"What did it look like?" Easter asks curiously, leaning towards me.

"The charm fit into my hand, and it looked very old," I began. "The moon was a tarnished silver with a brilliant blue stone in the middle. Flipping it over, I saw that there were marks on the back of the moon that I didn't understand. It looked like it was an engraving, but they weren't words or letters. As I inspected the charm; it grew warm and I swear that it started to sparkle."

"Sparkle?" Easter asks. "What do you mean?"

"Well I know it sounds silly, and when I asked Mom about it later, she called me a fool and grounded me for one whole month for touching it. Mom told me that it is just very old and she doesn't want it to get broken."

"I won't make fun of you," Easter promises.

Taking a deep breath, I press on, "Well when the charm began to feel warm, I flipped it over and looked into the stone and I could swear that it sparkled. Little lights appeared all over the inside of that stone. The lights were as small as pin pricks, but they were bright and some of them were different colors. Most were yellow, but some were red and blue. Then…" I paused, unsure.

"Please continue," Easter gushes excitedly.

"Well I know that this sounds crazy, but as I looked into the stone, I saw something move. It looked like a tiny shooting star. It crossed from one side of the stone and disappeared into the other side. It was the most beautiful thing I had ever seen." I looked at Easter, and her mouth was open in shock and her eyes were wide. "You don't believe me?" I ask her sadly.

Easter shut her mouth and stammered, "Um, no. I mean yes. I mean that can't be!"

"I know it sounds crazy," I admit. "But it happened. It wasn't a dream. When I saw that shooting star, I dropped the charm in surprise. That woke up my mom, and I have never been able to hold it again. Mom wears it on a chain around her neck when she sleeps now."

"It just can't be," Easter reflects. "That sounds like a Moon Stone, and no human should have one of those. And if it was a Moon Stone, why would it respond to you? No offense, Ana, but you are just a human."

Chapter Twenty - Moon Stones

I choose to ignore the "just a human" remark and ask, "What is a Moon Stone?" Looking thoughtful Easter answers, "They are brilliant, bright stones, and each one houses an entire universe. The hard-stone shell keeps the universe safe and protected, and it is the sacred duty of the moon to guard and keep all of the Moon Stones safe."

"Wait, universes?" I ask. "As in planets and a sun and…and people? That is impossible," I declare.

"No, Ana. It is very possible. I can just imagine the chaos that you caused when you dropped the stone." Looking me in the eye, Easter asks me, "Have you ever wondered what happened to the dinosaurs?"

"What? What do dinosaurs have to do with anything?" I ask in confusion.

"The moon was polishing the stones a long time ago when the Earth stone was dropped. It fell hard and the outer shell cracked. Dinosaurs," Easter divulges, "became extinct from that crack."

"What!?" I shriek. "How can that be? That is nonsense!"

"The crack allowed some cool air to rush in, and it started the Ice Age," Easter explains simply. "I am just thankful that the moon was able to repair the crack before all life forms became extinct. If he hadn't been able to, neither one of us would be here."

"Let's just say that Earth is in one of these Moon Stones," I volunteer sarcastically. "If we are in a Moon Stone, how can we have a Moon Stone? If there is an entire universe in one stone, the universe in my mother's stone would be…"

"Incredibly small," Easter replies. "Tiny. Those beings are invisible to our naked eye. We must use magic to distinguish them. Just like how we are too small for the larger beings to see us easily."

"What are you talking about?" I yell. "Are you suggesting there are giants?"

Tilting her head to one side thoughtfully, Easter replies, "Yes. Let us call them giants. But be nice. Keep in mind that we would be giants to the beings smaller than us."

I shake my head in disbelief, "I am sorry, but that all sounds pretty crazy."

"Is it as crazy as fairies and leprechauns were to you yesterday?" Easter asks me, smiling.

I smile back, "Yes! Yes, it all seems crazy!"

"But it is real. I am real."

"Yes, you are real. And if you are real, then maybe there are giants and Moon Stones and and, and…Santa Claus and Easter bunnies," I suggest, laughing in delight.

"Yes, Ana, and there is even more, and they are all wonderful," Easter agrees with twinkling eyes.

Laughing I admit, "I would love to meet them. I would love to meet all of them!"

Easter stops and looks at me seriously, "Really? Well that is interesting," she comments frowning.

Her serious expression stops my laughter, and I ask her, "What did you mean when you said that the Moon Stone 'responded' to me?"

"When you held it in your hand, you said that it sparkled and that you saw a shooting star, right?"

"Yes. At least that is what it looked like to me," I answer.

"It takes magic to power a Moon Stone enough for it to sparkle. And it takes a wish…a magic wish to cause a shooting star."

"I have heard that you should make a wish when you spot a shooting star," I suggest helpfully.

"Precisely," Easter agrees, nodding her head. "Shooting stars are caused by fairy wishes and powered by our magic. If you non-Fairy Folk, or NFFs, are lucky enough to observe a shooting star, you should make a wish in hopes that there is enough magic in that shooting star to make your wish come true, too."

"It sounds just like the story of Pinocchio where the Blue Fairy grants the wish that Geppetto made upon the shooting star!" I exclaim.

Blowing her breath out in a huff, Easter rolls her eyes, "THAT was the Leprechaun's doing. They thought it would be funny if the NFFs knew about the shooting star magic. After that story became popular, we never had so many humans wish so hard on shooting stars. Many of their wishes even came true!"

"Really?" I ask in disbelief.

"Really. We had to start using less magic to power the shooting stars after a boy wished he could talk to his dog, and it came true! My grandparents made the trip themselves to sort out that mess."

"What!?"

Smiling, Easter adds, "The boy was barking like a dog, and his parents were beside themselves with worry. His dog, however, appeared to really enjoy himself, and after the dog had a long conversation with the boy, that dog NEVER had dry dog food again. After that the boy gave his dog hot dogs every day to eat."

"T...talking...talking to dogs?" I stammer stupidly, my mind reeling. "That really happened?"

"But never mind that," continued Easter. "I have no idea how the Moon Stone was able to sparkle for you, and as far as the shooting star, that should have been impossible. It all should have been impossible."

Easter pauses lost in thought, then asks, "How in the world did your mother even get a Moon Stone?"

"I–I have no idea," I stammer earnestly. "Could my mom know what it is? Or does she just think it is a pretty stone?"

"I don't know," Easter remarks. "Did she ever tell you where it came from?"

"Not exactly," I replied, thinking hard. "She said that it was from her parents and that it was very old, so she didn't want us to touch it."

"Well, there is only one thing to do," Easter exclaims. "We must go visit Victoria and request that she grant you permission to speak with Stargazer."

"What, who?" I ask.

"You will see," Easter replies as she pulls her wand out again. With a flash and a few words that I cannot make out, there is a whooshing sound as a warm breeze hits us. I shut my eyes against the strong breeze, and when I open my eyes, we are no longer by the wicker furniture.

Chapter Twenty-one - Victoria

Looking around I realize that we are at a pond. The grass is green and lush, but we are not standing on the grass.

I scream in fear as the damp, rubbery surface beneath me bends under my weight and moves. I hear frogs chirp around us, and there are flowers everywhere.

"Are we on a giant lily pad!?" I scream in alarm.

Breathing fast I look for the shore. "I can't swim," I squeak in fear.

"No reason to be afraid, my dear," booms a loud voice.

Turning towards the voice, I am shocked to discover the largest fairy I have ever seen. She floats above us, above the water, and appears to be checking on the water lilies. She has bright pink, curly hair, and the top of her dress is bright white, but her dress skirt is what I mostly notice. It is gigantic and thick and a deep, deep green color.

"I am Victoria, the Amazonian Lily," the deep voice booms as she looks down at me. "What brings you and your guest here today, Easter?"

I am frozen in fear from being on the water and from having this giant looming over me. Bubble Gum is next to me and she baas and begins to happily stomp her hooves on the lily pad on which we stand.

I scream in fear, "Stop, Bubble Gum! Stop that! Please just stand still." I quickly sit down and tightly grip the side of the floating lily pad in terror. I am thankful that there is at least a tall rim around the perimeter of the lily pad. *At least I won't slide off and fall into the water,* I think.

But the goat must be trying to sink us! Ignoring my pleas to stand still, Bubble Gum never ceases to stomp, stomp, stomp. I am relieved when she jumps to the next giant lily pad, then the next one bleating happily.

Easter rises gracefully from our floating lily pad and flies towards Victoria. Leaning in she begins to whisper in Victoria's ear. They both glance at me, then back to each other, continuing their conversation.

I am too terrified to care that I am being ignored now that Bubble Gum is again on my lily pad. She is jumping and trying to make the water splash as the lily pad bounces in the water. Eventually Bubble Gum calms down and she begins chewing on some of the gigantic flowers floating nearby.

Relaxing I look around at my surroundings.

It was sunny when we were having tea, but here it is dusky, and stars shine in the sky. The full moon reflects brightly off of the water. Carefully I peer over the edge of the lily pad into the water and spot two big eyes looking at me from the water. *What could that be*, I wonder. I stare intently into the eyes as they rise to the surface and the head of a massive frog, as big as a car, comes into view. What in the world? I have never seen such a large frog. The massive frog opens its mouth and shouts a loud ribbit into my face. It is so loud that the water ripples and the lily pad floats away from the frog.

I grip the rim tightly as we bounce off the lily pad next to us. As the ripples clear, I make out something else in the water and lean over to discover monster-sized fish swimming happily beneath me. The fish remind me of the bright Koi fish that I had watched at the zoo, except they are definitely the biggest Koi I have ever observed. They appear to be the size of dolphins. The bright fish seem to dance in the water as they weave amongst the lily pads, flowers, and each other. I find myself admiring them, and I pet Bubble Gum on the neck when she comes next to me.

It is peaceful here, I think. The air is clean, and I inhale deeply. I hear a loud buzzing sound and look up from the water to discover mammoth dragonflies flying overhead. Their wings are bright emerald green and twinkle in the moonlight as they fly from flower to flower. I am not surprised to realize that they are as big as large dogs. Everything in this pond is gigantic.

I lie on my stomach and dip my fingers into the warm water as I admire the beauty of my surroundings. I gaze in fascination as the gigantic dragonflies perch gently on the edge of flowers, drink the nectar, then flit to the next. A fish swims to the surface and playfully spits water towards a dragonfly. I giggle in delight as the dragonfly immediately launches into the air to avoid getting wet.

Bubble Gum, who had been content next to me while I pet her neck, suddenly lowers her head and takes a large bite out of the rim of the lily pad.

Jumping up I pull her away from the lily pad and chastise her, "No, no, bad goat! Bad!"

She just looks at me as she pulls her head away from me and takes a bite out of the bottom of the lily pad. Water immediately flows in through the hole and begins to cover my feet. I scream out in terror as Bubble Gum bleats happily and starts jumping in the water, causing it to splash.

"Please help us," I cry out. "We are sinking!"

Easter and the giant Victoria stop their discussion, and Easter floats towards us, pulling her wand out as she approaches. I am on my hands and knees, frantically throwing handfuls of water out of the lily pad as quickly as I can. But the water is coming in much faster than I am throwing it out.

With a flick of her wrist, pink glitter flies out of Easter's wand and covers us. I shut my eyes to protect them from the dust. When I open my eyes, there is no water in the lily pad and there is no hole. I am not even wet! Looking at Bubble Gum, I smile to see that she has a bucket of flowers next to her that she is happily eating. Everything is perfect. *How does Easter do that*, I wonder.

Chapter Twenty-two - Water

Standing shakily on the moving, floating surface, I look up at Easter and Victoria and ask, "What is this place?"

Bending down the giant smiles at me and says, "I apologize, my dear. Again my name is Victoria the Amazonian Lily, and this is our Well Water."

"WELL water? This water is for drinking?" I ask in surprise, peering over the edge at the fish and the frogs in the pond.

The lily pad shudders as Victoria laughs so loudly and so deeply that flower petals fall from some of the flowers and I am knocked over by the force of her thunderous laugh.

"No, child," she responds, wiping tears away from her eyes. "This water is not for drinking. It is for making all things WELL. This is fairy water that is able to make you healthy, happy, and is able to solve problems. You are here so that we can solve the problem of how you got to be here. Now follow me," Victoria directs as she turns away from me, still chuckling.

Sitting up carefully on the lily pad, I begin to ask, "How do I..." But stop abruptly as the lily pad shifts and I am knocked backwards as it begins to move. I look around in fear, afraid that we are sinking again, but I find no hole.

Peering over the edge, I observe that one of the large fish has the stem of the lily pad in its mouth and is swimming after Victoria, pulling me along with it.

Bubble Gum baas in protest as her flower bucket tips over. Then she bites the bucket. Refusing to give in, Bubble Gum persists to chomp on the pail, and I can hear her teeth grinding as she tries unsuccessfully to eat the bucket as we follow Victoria.

I sit next to Bubble Gum and look towards Victoria.

Easter is flying alongside her, and I realize that Victoria is not actually floating above the water like I thought. Rather her dress is made from four of the large lily pads. They overlap each other at her waist, then fall heavily down her sides and rest upon the water. Victoria moves smoothly over the water , and I wonder if she can fly. *Maybe she is too large to fly*, I think. Or maybe the lily pads are attached to the water somehow and prevent her from taking flight.

As I am pondering this, I notice a small goat on the shore. It limps painfully towards the pond, carefully wades into the water, and lays down gently. After a moment, the goat stands up and walks easily out of the water. I am surprised to see that once on land, it begins to jump happily. It has no limp.

"Easter has told me that your parents warned you to stay away from the fence and the meadow. Do you know why, my dear?" Victoria asks, looking over her shoulder at me.

Still watching the now healthy little goat frolic on the shore, I shake my head and reply, "No. They wouldn't tell me anything."

"Interesting," she comments as we glide around a tree that is as tall as a skyscraper. My lily pad slows down as we slowly enter a lagoon. Coming out from beneath the branches of the gigantic tree, I take in the full moon above us, and directly below that full moon in the middle of the lagoon is an amazing waterfall.

"How can this be?" I ask in astonishment, looking up. There is no hill, cliff, or even rocks that the water falls from. The waterfall is so tall that I cannot make out the top. It looks as if the water is falling directly out of the sky. We make a wide circle around the waterfall, and sure enough, there is no structure on any side of the waterfall. The water spills straight down into the lagoon. And it is silent. The water is rushing fast, but all is silent. Where the falling water hits the lagoon surface, there is no splash, not even a ripple.

Fairies and animals are scattered around the gigantic waterfall, staring intently and silently into it. One fairy lands gently on the grass at the bank of the shore. She then jumps onto the closest giant lily pad, then the next. Slowly hopping closer to the waterfall.

"Why doesn't she just fly to the waterfall?" I whisper to Victoria.

"This is Moon Falls," Victoria explains. "It is a water bridge between our Fairy Realm and the Star Realm. The water comes directly from the moon who witnesses and knows all. Fairies are not allowed to cross the water bridge to the moon; flying is strictly prohibited."

We glide around the waterfall, and I scrutinize a fairy wearing a long, elegant, pink and white dress. She is flying gracefully between the waterfall and the fairies and other animals who sit around it.

"I thought you said flying was forbidden here?" I ask Victoria.

"Yes, it is forbidden to most. That is Stargazer Lily, and she is the keeper of Moon Falls. Only the Lily family is authorized to fly in this no-fly zone."

Stargazer notices us and flies closer. Her face and arms are covered with freckles, and she smiles warmly at us.

"Hello, Victoria, and my favorite niece, Easter."

Smiling, Easter replies, "I am your only niece, Aunt Stargazer."

"Never mind that, you would be my favorite, even if I had twenty nieces to pick from!" Then looking at me, she says warmly, "Welcome, Ana."

Chapter Twenty-Three - The Falls

Surprised I stand shakily on the lily pad and respond, "Hello. How did you know my name?"

Her voice is soft, and she laughs gently. "The moon and the stars speak to me, and they see and know everything. You have caused quite a bit of excitement over the past few days. All of the universes are gossiping about you and your sisters."

"They are?" I squeak. Stargazer takes my hand gently, and I feel myself rise off of the lily pad and float towards the waterfall. "Whoa! What is going on? How is this happening?" I ask as my feet kick in the air. I begin to panic as I leave the safety of the lily pad and hover over the water.

"I know that you can't swim, and everything is okay. I have you. Relax," Stargazer assures me.

Her voice is reassuring and calming. Holding her hand tightly, I cautiously look around me. We are approaching the waterfall, and I understand that the water itself isn't moving. Rather the water is a fixed object, but I can watch currents running underneath the clear surface. *Well that explains why there is no splash as it runs into the lagoon,* I think. I catch a glimpse of something in the current and squint to inspect it better. There it is again but different this time.

Studying the waterfall closely, I realize that I can make out pictures in the current. Many, many different pictures of different fairies and animals and humans. Watching them I am surprised that some of the pictures are moving.

"What is this?" I ask.

"Think of someone that you know," Stargazer suggests gently.

Immediately Becca pops into my mind. My little sister. *Where are you*, I wonder.

In the waterfall, an image grows brighter in the current of images and moves closer to me. I lean in and am astonished to discover Becca.

As I watch, Becca begins to move. She is surrounded by small creatures with huge, hairy ears and large hands.

They look like humans, except that their proportions are all wrong.

Their slender hands are as large as their bodies and their ears are pointed and as tall as their heads. The creatures have various hats atop their heads and fancy-looking shoes that curl up at their toes. They surround Becca, and everyone is laughing.

In fact the creatures all look to have permanent lines on their faces from smiling so much. Their smiles are so large on their faces and their dimples are so deep that it looks like that is how their expression is always, in everlasting grins. I am relieved to realize that Becca looks happy, too.

"How can this be?" I asked Stargazer. "Where is Becca?"

"Becca is exactly where you see her. Moon Falls can show you anyone that you want to view. There are billions of strands of knowledge in that current. Each one is capable of showing what a creature is doing now and what they have done in the past."

"Is that how she is RIGHT now? Am I watching her as she really is? She is okay?" I ask Stargazer anxiously.

"Yes, that is her right now, and you can deduce that she is fine."

"Who is she with? Who are those...little people?"

"Those are the Leprechauns that Becca is with," Stargazer answers me. "The whole universe has been cackling over their tricks over the past few days. Do you know what they did to Mrs. Beazley?"

Smiling widely Stargazer goes on before I can reply, "They hid one of EACH pair of her socks one night! In the morning, she had no matching socks AT ALL! Mrs. Beazley threw a horrible fit, yelling at her children and her husband. Oh, the neighbors will be talking about that for a while. She got so loud that one of the neighbors called the police and asked them to check and make sure that everything was all right. When that policeman knocked on her door, then she really got mad! What a frightful woman."

"Yes, she really is a terribly mean person," I announce. And I can't help but smile picturing her so upset. "What about someone who has died?" I ask nervously, thinking of Becca again. "Would you see dead people in the currents?"

"Yes, but your sister Becca is just fine," Stargazer replies reassuringly. "You saw her as she is. To take a peek at someone who has passed; you just have to think of someone who you know has passed away," Stargazer instructs me.

"I have always wondered what my grandparents look like," I admit slowly. "I have never met them because Mother says that they died before I was born. May I please view my mother's parents, my grandparents?" I ask Stargazer.

Smiling kindly Stargazer replies, "I am not in charge of what Moon Falls shows. I myself do not know what will be revealed until I ask. Sometimes you might get something unexpected, but the moon and stars know all there is to know. They have been here before us and they will be here after us. Please just ask them, and they will show you what you seek."

Turning towards the waterfall, I look through the clear , unmoving shell at the ripples of color flowing quickly underneath. Clearing my throat, I recite clearly to the waterfall, "Would you please show me my mother's parents, my grandparents?"

There is a hum, and I spot a light in the center of the Falls. It grows brighter and brighter as it slowly comes closer. I wince as it intensifies and I cover my eyes from the glare.

"This is a very old memory," Stargazer comments. "It is taking a lot of energy for the moon to reveal it. Someone must have tried to forget this memory for it to be so well-hidden. They wished it away for a long time. "

"Who would have done that?"

"I am afraid that I do not know the answer to that question. But it is a very important thing for you to know, this memory is."

"What? Why do you say that?" I ask her while shutting my eyes in addition to having them covered against the light.

"The more important the image or memory is to the viewer, the brighter it is. And this is the most blinding memory I have ever seen. Here, put this on over your head, so that you can make out what the moon is showing you," Stargazer tells me, handing me something.

Keeping my eyes shut, I run my hands over the object from Stargazer. It is heavy and smooth and...and round. "What is this?" I ask her.

"It is an orb that will protect your eyes from the light. Keep your eyes shut and put it over your head. Then you may open your eyes and what you requested will be revealed."

It feels like a fishbowl, I think as I pull the object over my head and impatiently open my eyes. I wince from the bright light. It is not blinding like before but still very bright. As my eyes adjust, images began to form in the bright current.

I gawk at a little man and a little lady. They don't look anything like my other grandparents who have white hair, wrinkles, and glasses. This couple looks young and healthy.

My grandfather has an orange suit on. The jacket is long in the back, and the material is shiny and is covered with black dots. My grandmother has a matching shiny, odd-looking dress on. It is made of the same material as my grandfather's suit and is tight at her waist and shoulder less.

Her top is a light orange and individual strands with rounded tops circle around her waist and curl up to just under her chin. Her skirt balloons out at her hips before falling around her legs. Her skirt is a dark orange, and there are black dots scattered around her waist then fading off as they cascade down her skirt. The little man is holding her arm and they are...FLYING!

My mouth falls open in surprise, and I scream. They have wings fluttering from their backs. I feel like I might faint. Which is not good since we are hovering above water and I cannot swim.

Stargazer grabs me, so that I don't fall, and states very quietly, "Those are the Tigers."

"What? Do you know them?" I gasp.

Stargazer nods. "Those are the Tigers. Tiger Lilys that is."

My mouth falls open, "Are they part of your Royal Fairy family?"

Looking serious, Stargazer answers, "Yes. They are my parents."

Easter had been floating silently behind us, but now rushes forward and looks at the bright image in the current. "Those are MY grandparents. Maybe the Falls misunderstood since I am right here. Why don't you try asking again," she suggests in a shaky voice.

"Yes, that cannot be right. The Tigers only had Royal and I, so they cannot be your grandparents. And you are a human. You don't even have wings!"

Looking at Moon Falls, I clear my throat and request loudly, "May I, Ana, please see MY grandparents? My mother's parents...please."

The current image fades, and another image begins to grow in the deep current.

Stargazer sighs in relief and exclaims, "I knew it had to be a mistake. That was good thinking, Easter, thank you."

I never take my eyes from the light that is growing brighter and brighter as it moves towards the edge of the Falls into our view. I still have my protective orb on my head, protecting my eyes, but I find myself squinting anyway against the light.

"This memory is even brighter than the last one," Stargazer cries in alarm. "Here, take this also," she orders as she quickly places something else over my eyes in addition to the orb. The light dims as another shade of protection is put between my eyes and the light, but it is still blinding.

I am so excited and nervous to see my grandparents that I am shaking. I take a deep breath and force myself to stay still. That is when I realize that I am not actually shaking, rather everything around me seems to be shaking.

Stargazer holds my left arm firmly, and I feel Easter grasp my right arm hard. I look at her and notice that her eyes are wide in disbelief. The water below the Falls is rippling, and waves are forming below us. I glimpse fairies and goats fall off of their lily pads into the water from the force.

A wave collides with the lily pad that Bubble Gum is on, and the little goat falls off into the water. I look frantically for her and then spy her head bob up to the surface. She happily starts swimming and spitting water up in the air.

I am relieved that she is okay, and now I am happy that I am above the water. Whatever is happening, I feel safer with Easter and Stargazer at my side, even if I am up in the air looking at a blinding light and being jostled around by some invisible force. *What is going on*, I wonder. Raising my head again, I stare into the approaching light.

My teeth are chattering from the vibrations coming from the Falls, and we are actually being pushed back and forth in the air. I can feel Easter and Stargazer fighting against the wind to keep us in place. *How long can they hold us here*, I wonder.

"Look," Stargazer commands. "This is important."

Obediently I focus on the light and can make out movement in the current. People dressed in orange. With a lump in my throat, I realize that it is the same shade of orange as the Tigers had been wearing.

"It can't be," Easter whispers.

The picture becomes clearer, and I can definitely identify that the couple in Moon Falls are the Tigers.

"Somehow it must be," Stargazer observes. "I don't know how, but Moon Falls is never wrong. The Tiger Lilys are your grandparents, Ana."

"Maybe your mom was adopted..." Easter trails off, thinking out loud.

Before anyone could say anything more, the vibration grows even more intense, and I start to feel sick to my stomach from the aggressive midair shaking that we are getting.

The Tigers are moving in the image. They have similar matching outfits on as before, but they are close to each other and looking downwards. Our view moves down also, and I hear Easter and Stargazer gasp of disbelief when we recognize that Mrs. Tiger Lily is holding a small baby. Dark hair is peeking out from the blanket wrapped around the baby, and the Tigers are smiling at the baby in happiness.

I wince in pain as a thunderous crack booms all around us as the image supernovas into the brightest flash that I have ever witnessed. The three of us are thrown back through the air.

Plummeting towards the ground, I see the image of the Tigers darken and flicker. Then the rest of the Falls begin to flash. As I land in the cool water surrounding the Falls, I think, *my grandparents were fairies!*

Chapter Twenty-Four - Aftermath

*O*pening my eyes slowly, I moan as I move my arms to try to sit up. My entire body aches, and it feels as if I have just been run over by a truck. I painfully look around and take notice of the chaos. There are wet goats and fairies all around me. I am on the edge of the lagoon, and everyone is staring up into the sky. Their faces are sad and worried. Looking up I see Stargazer flying frantically around Moon Falls, which now has a giant crack down the side of it.

There is no longer a current of images flowing continuously in the water. Now it is dark, except for the occasional crackling sound and a brief flash of light. It reminds me of when a battery is weak in a flashlight. The light comes on for a moment, but it is weak and almost immediately disappears.

I feel a soft hand on my shoulder and smell something refreshing.

"Are you alright, miss?" a kind voice asks me. Turning towards the voice, I discover a gentle-looking boy fairy dressed all in green next to me, and I recognize the scent.

"Are you a Peppermint?" I asked him.

"Yes, I am indeed a Peppermint. At your service, ma'am," he volunteers, giving me a light bow. "You had quite a nasty fall," he continues, motioning towards something shattered on the ground.

Looking at what he is pointing at, my stomach flips when I realize it is the orb that Stargazer had placed upon my head and it is cracked in half! That could have been my skull split into two pieces. I think in panic and then feel woozy at the thought.

"Uh, oh. Calm down, miss. Lay back and have a drink of this to help yourself relax," the Peppermint suggests, pulling a pillow out from thin air and placing it behind my back. Then he pulls a cup of something steaming in a dainty teacup from the air also. I allow him to settle me against the pillow, and I carefully take the steaming cup from him. Bringing it up to my nose, I inhale and look at the Peppermint.

"Drink up," he encourages me. "It is hot Peppermint tea. It will have you up and about in no time!"

I spy other Peppermints offering tea and comfort to other fairies and I even notice Bubble Gum chewing happily on a bunch of green leaves with a Peppermint softly petting her.

"What are you giving the goats?" I ask.

"Peppermint leaves," he answers. "Oh, they love them. Now go on, drink up please. I am not a good Peppermint if I don't help you to feel better."

I raise the teacup to my lips and take a small drink, then smile happily. "It is delicious," I exclaim and thirstily gulp the rest down.

Smiling happily the Peppermint offers, "Have as much as you'd like." And my glass immediately refills to the top.

I drink some more, then ask, "What happened?"

Sighing heavily the Peppermint shakes his head in disbelief and replies quietly, "I don't know all of the details, but we received an emergency call for the Peppermint Patrol. I was taking a nap when I woke up to the most alarm calls I have ever heard at one time before."

"How did anyone call you?" I interrupt, looking around for a phone.

Looking at me strangely, the Peppermint responds, "Mentally of course. Using the Peppermint Express."

"Do you mean that you can hear thoughts?" I ask him in disbelief.

"What other way is there?" he asks me. Then he looks at my back, and a look of pity comes over his face. "Oh, you are the human that Easter is visiting with, aren't you? You seem so much like a fairy, and this is all so upsetting that I failed to notice your lack of wings. My apologies, ma'am. Humans are forced to use machines to communicate like the...the...telephone is that what it is called, ma'am." I nod and he resumes, "Fairies use the Peppermint Express to call for help. Any fairy who needs assistance simply thinks Peppermint, then their message. All of the Peppermints who are on duty receive the message instantly. In our minds, we both hear the words of the message and witness what that fairy sees. Each message also has a location attached to it, so that we know EXACTLY where that fairy is."

"Can fairies communicate to non-Peppermints that way? Using their mind, I mean," I ask curiously.

Puffing out his chest in pride, he states, "Absolutely! Fairies have the most evolved, efficient, and quick Express system there has ever been. Fairies can contact the Gladiolas for protection or the Goat Beards for anything having to do with our goats to name a few."

"Amazing," I declare.

"Anyway," the Peppermint adds. "I knew it was the most important matter because I was receiving the message, even though I wasn't on duty. I don't recall that ever happening before, so I was immediately alarmed. Then to receive so many calls for help at the same time was even more concerning! I jumped out of bed and immediately started getting dressed while reviewing the incoming messages. Everyone was saying that there had been an accident at Moon Falls and the Falls were actually BROKEN. That no one could find their loved ones in the Falls. Hearing this many of us had to take some Peppermint tea ourselves before we could even leave to calm ourselves. Imagine, no Moon Falls!" he cries in astonishment. "Why that is how we check on our relatives when they are away and that is how we show our children who their ancestors were and what our history is. I don't know how I am going to show my own little Peppermints our proud history and how the Peppermint Patrol began and evolved into the finest healing squad in the Realms."

At this he looks like he might begin to cry. Reaching out I wrap my arms around him and give him a reassuring hug.

Sniffling he apologizes, "I am here to help you feel better, not the other way around."

"It's alright," I guarantee him. "Everyone needs a hug sometimes. What happens now that Moon Falls is broken?"

Sniffling, the Peppermint pulls away and looks around at the chaos. Looking up he points at Stargazer and replies, "I guess I don't know. This has never happened before, but I know that Stargazer will be able to fix it. I just wonder what could have caused this. Oh, wait a minute. Here we are," he mutters distractedly. Putting a hand to his head, he says relieved, "Easter and her mother are preparing a News Express about this accident right now."

"How do you know that?" I ask him surprised.

"I just received a News Express Alert announcing it. I also received a Personal Express from Easter asking me to escort you to her. Is that okay with you, ma'am?"

"Yes, and please call me Ana."

"Alright, Miss Ana. Please follow me this way," he announces.

I allow him to pull me to my feet and I look around for Bubble Gum. I feel something cold and wet press against my arm and jump in surprise. Looking down I find Bubble Gum calmly chewing on a mouthful of leaves and looking up at me expectantly. I reach down and scratch her chin. She closes her eyes and leans into me, completely enjoying the attention.

The Peppermint suggests, "Please follow me this way."

I stop petting Bubble Gum, and she immediately snaps her eyes open and baas at me in protest. Leaves falling from her mouth as she does.

Smiling at her, I suggest, "Come along, Bubble Gum. Let's go find Easter."

Her ears perk up at Easter's name and she wags her stubby tail excitedly and begins to follow me.

The Peppermint pulls out his red and white striped wand and twirls it above our heads, speaking softly. Green leaves fall from the end of his wand and fall down upon us, glittering in the moonlight. I close my eyes against the ticklish leaves and am not surprised that I am no longer near Moon Falls when I open them.

Chapter Twenty-Five – Pixie Palace

The first thing I hear are voices, a lot of voices. They are talking excitedly and loudly, and they sound frantic. I open my eyes and take in a great, breathtaking room. The walls are covered with more flowers than I have ever seen in my life. I inhale deeply and enjoy the strong scent of lily and rose and lilac to name a few. The smell is heavenly.

The floor feels soft, and I look down to realize that I am standing on thick green moss. Raising my head, I see that the wall in front of me is covered completely in roses of all different shapes and colors and sizes. The only thing that breaks up the wall is an intricate stained-glass window depicting fairies emerging from giant roses. My eyes gaze upward in an attempt to take in the majesty of this room, and I squeal in delight when I notice that there is no ceiling! Instead I can make out the clear blue sky with just a few fluffy clouds scattered here and there. Fairies are flying down into the room and landing gracefully wherever there is room.

The area is shoulder to wing packed with fairies, goats, and small, big-eared, odd-looking leprechauns. Some of the fairies around me appear quite commonly dressed while others are so exquisite that I can't help but to gap at them. One tall fairy has her white hair curled and the curls extravagantly piled on top of her head, all of which is further adorned with a sprinkle of sparkling jewels. I bend my neck back as far as I can attempting to determine how tall her hair is and think I am glad that they do not have ceilings here.

Another fairy bumps into me as he flutters past. He is in a dirty blue shirt and brown pants, both of which are torn. His hair is long and wild, and as he passes me, I am shocked to notice a bird's nest atop of his head complete with a family of small birds chirping inside. In his haste, he collides into another fairy, which causes the larger bird to tumble from the nest. Flitting furiously the bird flies in front of the hasty fairy on whose head their family is perched and tweets angrily in front of his face. I can't hear if the fairy responded and cannot glimpse his face in the crowd as the crowd is so large. But I do observe him slow, and the small bird quickly rejoins his family in the nest. Staring after them in bewilderment, I scream when someone grabs my shoulder.

"AWWW, what!?" I scream as I feel hands on my shoulders, turning me around, and I am relieved that it is Easter.

"I was so worried after the explosion that I called a Peppermint right away!" Easter is saying. "But this is such an emergency that I had to rush back to the palace. I am sorry; do you forgive me for leaving you?"

"Yes, yes. Of course," I stutter.

"And are you feeling better?" she asks.

"Yes, the Peppermints are amazing! He made me feel much better. They have quite the magic touch."

At this Easter smiles. "Yes, they definitely do have the magic touch when it comes to helping one feel better. That is what they do best."

"Where are we?" I ask her. "This is the MOST beautiful place I have ever been."

Smiling, Easter replies, "This isn't a place."

"What? What do you mean?" I ask her dumbly.

"THIS is not a place. This is the PALACE!" Easter announces dramatically. "Welcome to Pixie Palace! The most AMAZING, FABULOUS PALACE in all of the Realms! This room is the Fantastic Fairy room where each wall is dedicated to one of the fairy families." She sweeps her arm out behind her as she speaks, and I look over her shoulder to scan the room and realize it is even larger than I had initially thought.

The room extends for as far as I can see.

"The next room over is the Lucky Leprechaun, which is entirely dedicated to you know who," Easter declares, winking. Ticking a finger up as she names each one, she states, "Then there is Fancy Fish, Honey Bee Haven, Proud Pegasus, Distinguished Dignitaries, and the Celestial Seascape just to name a few. I bet you can guess who each room is for."

I nod slowly. "Yes, all of them except for one. Who are the Distinguished Dignitaries? That sounds like it would be for royalty or the Supreme Rulers?"

"Oh, that is the goat room," Easter replies simply.

I choke in surprise, "What!?"

Shrugging, Easter informs me, "The goats go by DD for short. So technically when you talk to Bubble Gum, her proper name is Distinguished Dignitary Bubble Gum. But she must like you because she doesn't seem to mind you not using her full DD name."

"What? Well, well...I...um...I didn't know," I stutter while looking at the gangly little goat next to us.

"No worries, Ana," Easter replies. "We must talk about what happened."

"Okay," I agree as Easter motions me to follow her. "The Tigers are my grandparents. If they are yours also, that would make us related."

"We would be cousins," I reply.

"Yes, but how can that be? I am a fairy while you are a NFF! And as far as I know, the Tigers only have two children."

"Your mom and Stargazer, right?" I ask.

"Exactly. I think the best way to discover if there is any truth to this is to talk with the Tigers. After our announcement, I think we should visit them. Okay?"

"Sounds good."

"It's settled then," Easter states.

We hear a murmur in the crowd, and I look up to find Stargazer entering the room. "Please wait here for me. I will be back as soon as I can. I must address the Realm with my mother and Stargazer," Easter explains as she hurries away from me.

I sigh and shake my head in disbelief as I watch her gracefully fly away. *How can this be happening*, I wonder. I am no fairy. And I am definitely not related to any royalty. I must be the most awkward, clumsy person ever. *No, there is definitely no royal blood in me*, I think. No matter how cool that might be to be a delicate, magical fairy, I am just not. No, I am just a normal girl.

The room silences, and I look up to catch sight of Easter and Stargazer standing next to a regal-looking fairy. The top of her dress is a bright yellow, tight at the waist with a full-length white skirt. She has golden hair that is curled and pinned up around a dazzling crown. Her face is smooth and timeless.

Her skin is the color of white cream and her lips are a soft pink. This must be Easter's mom, Royal, I think. Facing the gathering of fairies, the golden-haired fairy begins to speak.

"Hello, my fellow fairies, leprechauns, and friends. My daughter, Stargazer and I address you today on a most urgent matter. As many of you already know, there was an accident today at Moon Falls. While no one was badly injured, Moon Falls is currently in need of repairs and is not functioning."

At this there was a gasp from the gathered assembly, and a few of the women and children began to cry quietly.

Her face strong and her voice steady, Royal continues, "This has never happened before, but we have asked the best in the Realms to assist Stargazer with repairs. These repairs have already begun, and I ask all of you to remain calm and carry on with everything as normal. I know you must have many questions and I will try my best to answer some of the more urgent ones. But first, tomorrow's Small Sprite's field trip to Moon Falls is cancelled until further notice. Moon Falls and the Well Water are both temporarily off limits while repairs are being done."

"Excuse me, My Lady. I beg your forgiveness, but I need to ask. Was this caused by the…the…Banshee," a nervous-looking fairy in the crowd asks meekly.

There was a piercing gasp of shock in the room at this, and a child began to cry loudly. The assembled crowd murmured to each other, and no one observed, or cared, that the child was crying. Everyone seemed to hold their breath, awaiting Royal's response.

"Mind your words!" Royal snaps harshly. "There is no need to cause a panic!"

"I beg your forgiveness, Supreme Ruler," the woman pleads. "But I need to know. If I can tell my little ones it was caused by something else, they will sleep soundly and not have night terrors."

Sighing, Royal looks glumly at the crowd. "We have no evidence that this horrible tragedy had anything to do with the Banshee."

"What do you know about what happened?" another fairy asks.

"We know that the terrible accident was caused by a memory," Royal states.

The crowd looks surprised. "How could that break Moon Falls?" a tall, blue fairy in the crowd questions.

"I know it sounds impossible," Royal admits. "My own daughter was there at the time and she witnessed it."

"It is true," Easter announces loudly. "I was there while Stargazer was assisting someone to discover memories."

"Well we have all done that before," the tall fairy said, sounding bewildered. "That is one of the purposes of Moon Falls. I can't imagine that a memory would have done anything."

"This memory was different. It was...forgotten," Stargazer adds. "More than forgotten, it was hidden. Someone wished it to be forgotten forever."

"Why would someone do that?" an elderly fairy asks. "And who did it?"

"I am afraid that we do not have those answers yet," Royal replies. "But I assure you that we will. The important thing is that no one was seriously injured during the incident. Now please don't worry about this any longer. Go about everything as normal with one exception; please stay away from Moon Falls and the Well Water while the repairs are occurring. I will let everyone know when I know more. Thank you and be brave," Royal declares in a low voice while raising her wand in the air above her head.

Every other fairy raises their wand above their own head and faces Royal in unison. Glitter twinkles down from the wands and falls gently onto the crowd.

"None of us are alone," Royal promises. "Together we are strong. Be well, my friends," Royal proclaims kindly and lowers her wand.

The crowd appears to be reassured. There are now smiles on some of the faces, and I am happy that I don't detect anyone crying anymore.

Easter whispers in her mother's ear, and I see Royal lift her head and scan the room.

Her eyes find mine, and I know they are talking about me. Royal nods at something that Easter says, then they both straighten and face me. They look very serious, and I feel my spine stiffen in apprehension. Slowly they begin to move through the crowded room, responding to fairies as they go. They pause to answer a question from a nervous-looking Leprechaun, wringing a very worn hat in his hands as he shuffles from foot to foot, and Royal gives a scared-looking child a tender hug.

Reaching me they stop, and Royal looks me directly in the eye and asks, "So you are the human that I have been hearing so much about."

Chapter Twenty-Six – Royal

"Yes, yes, I suppose I must be," I stammer.

"You have made a horrible mess of things today. The fairies are almost in a panic, and every member of the Peppermint Patrol is working overtime right now attempting to calm everyone. Come clean, young lady, how did you do it?"

"W…what?" I ask fearfully. "How did I do what, Mrs. Supreme Ruler… Your Grace…Your Highness…" I stutter, feeling completely intimidated by her. I feel myself shaking in fear and try to calm and stand still and to be brave.

"Call me Royal," she commands. Looking at me, she relaxes and gently puts her hand on my shaking shoulder. "Calm yourself," she instructs me. "Please, let's start from the beginning at the meadow. The Guardian informs me that when he inspected you, he sensed the aura of the Fairy Realm and thus allowed you to cross."

"When he inspected me?" I squeak. "When did he inspect me?"

At this Royal smiles just a little. "Did he sniff you?" she asks me.

I think hard, trying to remember. "Yes, I do remember that he sniffed my hand before accepting our sugar cube."

Frowning, Royal said to me, "Do you mean to tell me that he accepted your bribe? That you offered him sugar and that he accepted?"

"Y…yes. We knew that he liked sugar and we thought it might calm him down. He appeared agitated that we crossed the fence and were in the meadow."

"As he should have been since he is supposed to protect us. But how did you know that he liked sugar?" Royal demanded.

"Well, uh. I mean, from when we had given him sugar before. From the other side of the fence, we would give him sugar cubes through the rails."

Royal's eyes widen at this, and she speculates quietly, "Interesting…He will have to be spoken to for that."

"What? Why? I didn't mean to get him into trouble," I assert quickly.

"Sugar is strictly forbidden for horses," Easter tells me helpfully. "They find it irresistible, and if they become addicted to sugar, they will do most anything for it."

Nodding slightly Royal adds, "I am very surprised that our Guardian would be so weak as to accept sugar bribes. He should be the strongest horse in the Realm."

"Isn't that how Banshee misled Pegasus?" Easter asks her mom.

Sadness overcomes Royal's face, and she replies quietly, "Yes."

Turning towards me, Royal Explains, "Our beloved Pegasus was a faithful, dear friend of mine until Banshee introduced him to sugar. He became so addicted that he would do anything that she asked as long as she kept giving him that delicious sugar. No one knew that Pegasus had that weakness until Banshee discovered it and used it to her advantage. Unfortunately it has the same effect on horses as it does on Pegasus since they are such a close relation," Royal finishes sadly.

Easter bursts out, "Allowing strangers into our realm without notifying us AND eating sugar! Why is our Guardian acting so weirdly?"

"Could it be that the sugar is affecting him?" I ask gently. "Would that make him behave strangely?" I volunteer helpfully, trying to lessen the seriousness I would hate for that beautiful horse to be in trouble because of me, I think.

"Perhaps," Royal considers thoughtfully while tapping her slender pointer finger against her chin and looking into the distance, obviously deep in thought over their Guardian. Her lips were pressed so tightly together that they seemed to have lost their color and were almost as pale as her skin. She looked so worried that I was overcome with guilt.

"I am so sorry!" I blurt out suddenly. I never meant to harm your Guardian! He is so beautiful, and I just wanted I just wanted…wanted to see…" I trail off miserably.

"Now, now, girl," Royal remarks gently. "You didn't know. We will talk with him further and try to understand what is happening. We will keep him under close surveillance for now." Looking at me, Royal commands, "Please, tell me what else has happened?"

I take a deep breath and decide to disclose EVERYTHING. I begin with when my sisters and I saw the meadow, bumping into Easter, meeting Salvia, my run in with Glad, and finally what I had witnessed at Moon Falls.

When I am done, I look at Royal and recognize disbelief on her face. Her large, sparkling eyes look too big for her face, and they have grown even larger after listening to my story. They glimmer with confusion. She manages a small smile and blinks rapidly.

Looking curiously at me, she admits, "That is an amazing story. If Easter wasn't here to support it, I don't know that I would believe it.

"I saw the Tigers, too, Mom", Easter contributes. "I don't know how that is possible, but they appeared when Ana AND Stargazer asked to view Ana's grandparents. Has the Falls ever been wrong, Mom?"

"As far as I know, Moon Falls has never been inaccurate," Royal replies. "I honestly don't understand it either."

"I told Ana that I think we should visit the Tigers and ask them about this," Easter continues.

"Yes," Royal agrees. She pulls her sparkling clear wand from out of the air and declares, "Let us make a visit to the Tigers immediately."

She delicately waves the wand above our heads and whispers something that I can't make out, but the words are spoken so softly and sweetly that what I can hear sounds like music.

Small stars cascade all around us from her wand. They are so plentiful that I began to lose sight of anything else. I reach my hand out nervously and grasp Easter's hand. Easter gives me a reassuring smile and squeezes my hand gently just before she disappears into the storm of stars. Then all around me are sparkling silver stars. I feel a slight breeze tickle my arms, then a bump upon my feet, signaling that we have arrived at our destination.

The stars vanish, and I realize that we are in a lovely meadow. It is filled with flowers and songbirds. I listen to birds chirp and whistle while they sing, and I can just make out the rippling sound of a nearby stream. *Are the Tigers here*, I wonder as I look around.

Chapter Twenty-Seven - The Tigers

"Mum, Dad, I apologize for coming unannounced, but I must speak with you," Royal calls out loudly.

I hear a faint rustle and look up to notice two fairies emerging from a very large orange Tiger Lily flower.

Their glorious matching orange outfits are covered with yellow dust, and they smile warmly when they glimpse us. I recognize them from the Falls instantly and break out into a cold, nervous sweat. *Are these my grandparents*, I wonder.

"Welcome, my dears!" Mr. Tiger greets us.

"Please pardon our mess," Mrs. Tiger apologizes. "You caught us in the middle of pollinating the flowers."

Royal flies towards them, returning their warm smiles and embraces them tightly. "Never mind some pollen dust," she replies kindly. "What fun is being a fairy if you can't get dirty every now and then? I am happy to see you, Mum and Dad."

"Well of course we are happy to have you here again, too, my dear. It has been too long!" Mrs. Tiger declares.

"Why don't you visit us more often?" she demands of Royal, withdrawing from her embrace to put her hands firmly on her hips and stare seriously into her face. Everyone is silent for a moment, then the two fairies both throw their heads back in delight and laugh gleefully. The flowers surrounding them glow brightly and stand up taller at this.

Gasping, I rub my eyes, then look again. *It can't be*, I think. I must be imagining it. But now the flowers are definitely glowing. As their laughter slows, the flowers dim and return to normal.

Wiping tears from the corners of her perfect eyes, Royal giggles, "Yes, Mum. Breakfast this morning was far too long a time to be away from you both."

"Far, far too long!" Mrs. Tiger agrees dramatically. "We missed you for lunch! What do you have to say for yourself not to have lunch with us? It's as if you have a Realm to rule!"

What brings you back to our meadow today?" Mr. Tiger inquires. Then noticing me, he pauses. "Do we know you, young lady?" he quizzes me. "You look familiar."

Shyly I step forward and look up at them. "I was hoping that you could tell me," I admit quietly with a slight tremble in my voice. Taking a deep breath to try to calm down , I ask, "Do you know my mother? Her name is Night."

At this a look of shock and terror replace the smiles on their faces. Mrs. Tiger utters a small moan as her head drops to one side, and she tumbles right out of the sky towards the ground.

"My dear!" Mr. Tiger calls out in panic as he flies to her side. Catching her in his arms. Mr. Tiger shakes her gently and pleads, "Wake up. I have you. You will be okay."

Royal calls out, "Please, would someone call a Peppermint?" and she and Easter both rush forward to help. I am left behind with Bubble Gum. The small goat looks at me uncaring and struts over to a nearby rose bush. Without hesitation she plunges her head into the bush and begins noisily eating. Rose petals, leaves, and twigs fly everywhere. Shaking my head, I look back towards the fairies.

A Peppermint arrives from out of nowhere and sits Mrs. Tiger up comfortably with pillows behind her back. After having a cup of peppermint tea, Mrs. Tiger looks at me and motions me to come forward. I nervously move closer.

"I am alright," Mrs. Tiger is reassuring a Peppermint. "Really, all of this fuss over an old lady taking a fall. This is embarrassing. Please, let us welcome our guest." She motions me to come even closer, and as I approach, I detect tears in her eyes. Upon arriving at her side, Mrs. Tiger reaches out and pulls me in for a tight hug. With her arms around me, she whispers, "Night's daughter…Night's daughter," while stroking my hair.

Mr. Tiger clears his throat and remarks, "Darling. I think you are scaring her." At this she pulls away from me, and I see shock on Royal's face.

"Mum, what is going on?" Royal demands.

"Yes," I request quietly. "Do you know me, Mrs. Tiger?"

Taking a deep breath while never taking her eyes off of me, Mrs. Tiger replies, "Please, my dear, call me Grams."

Chapter Twenty-Eight – Truth

My mouth falls open in surprise. But it is Royal who screams out, "What!? MOTHER, how can this be?"

Easter starts to laugh and clarifies, "Do you mean that I have a cousin? I have ALWAYS wanted a cousin!"

Tears running down her cheeks, Mrs. Tiger, or Grams I suppose, replies, "Yes, Easter, you have a cousin. Actually maybe more than one; do you have any siblings, dear?" she asks me.

"Y…y…yes. Yes, I have two sisters," I spit out finally.

"Fabulous! Are they here with you?"

"Oh, yes. I am so sorry. We separated them until we could understand better what was going on. Let me call them here," Easter volunteers eagerly. "I cannot wait to meet my other cousins!"

Easter twirls her wand excitedly through the air, causing pink dust to fly everywhere in her excitement. It grows thicker and thicker and then I pick up familiar voices. I hear Lizzie and Becca!

Lizzie is talking quickly and excitedly, but I cannot understand the words. She sounds very far away but happy. Then I pick up Becca's voice, quiet at first, then louder and louder.

Becca is giggling. The giggle grows more distinct and then I can make out her splendid laugh! Oh, how I have missed her laugh I realize. Their voices grow louder and sharper, and as the dust clears, I am overjoyed to recognize both of my sisters in front of me.

Lizzie has a delicate book that looks as if it was made from dry, flattened flowers and an old-fashioned, fancy feather pen in her hand. The feather is huge and a bright flashy blue color. The feather flops around crazily as Lizzie writes furiously in her flower notebook. Her hair is tucked behind her ears, and she is so focused on whatever she is working on that I don't think she is aware that I am here.

Becca, on the other hand, is sitting on the ground holding her belly. She is laughing so hard that tears stream down her cheeks. The loud laughter finally causes Lizzie to look up and she and I both gawk in surprise at Becca.

Becca is a mess. She is covered in…socks. Blues, green, oriental, thick warm winter socks and thin dress socks. Socks of all different colors and sizes are tangled in her hair, on her clothes, and even coming out of her pockets. I am too stunned to move. They both look happy and healthy, but where have they been? My thoughts are interrupted as I am shoved aside by Bubble Gum.

Baaing excitedly Bubble Gum races towards Becca, jumps up, and snags a black dress sock off of her shoulder. She begins to quickly eat the sock and grabs at a lime green sock sticking out from Becca's pocket, almost losing the first sock while doing so.

"Oh, hello, little goat," Becca says in surprise. "Where did you come from?" Scratching Bubble Gum on her neck, Becca looks up and spots me. She jumps up quickly and screams, "ANA, ANA, ANA! I am SO happy to see you!"

She rushes towards me, tripping over Bubble Gum in her enthusiasm, and she and the goat both tumble to the ground in a tangled mess of socks, fur, and feet. Bubble Gum is baaing and thrashing her hooves in the air wildly as she tries to stand. Becca looks ridiculously similar to the goat as her feet slip and slide in the mound of socks as she tries to get up.

Lizzie giggles as they struggle to get untangled from their mess.

"LIZZIE!" Becca screams angrily. "How long have you been here? Where did you two go? Why did you leave me alone? Why aren't you helping me out of this, this, this mess?" Becca demands.

We both step forward to help untangle the two, and Becca gushes, "I have so much to tell you. Oh, you won't believe what I have done and who I have met! Do you remember the old Mrs. Beazley?" Becca asks with a snort. "Boy, did she get a surprise!" Grabbing my hand to pull herself up, Becca notices the Lily Family surrounding us. "Oh, hello. I am Becca. Who are you?" Becca asks the fairies. The Lilys look at each other smiling, but before they can answer, Becca throws her arms around me and pulls me in for a tight hug. "Whoever they are, if they are friends of Ana and Lizzie, they are friends of mine."

Grabbing Lizzie quickly in a tight hug, Becca asks her, "Who are your new friends?"

"Uh, um…I am afraid that I…I don't know. I just got here, too," Lizzie responds.

Becca whips her head towards me and shrieks, "YOU left Lizzie alone? Here in an unknown place! Anything could have happened to her!"

I put my hand on my hips and look at my little sister, "May I remind you, Becca, that YOU are my younger sister, not Lizzie," I observe sweetly.

"Well that is even worse!" Becca declares hotly. "You abandoned your little sister AND your big sister!"

Easter turns to Royal and cries excitedly, "I think I am going to like them!"

Hearing this Lizzie, Becca and I turn towards the Lilys, and Lizzie inquires, "I am sorry, have we met?"

Stepping forward Easter sticks out her perfect, elegant hand to Becca. With her neon pink fingernail polish glittering in the sunlight, she responds, "I am Easter Lily, and this is our family, the Lilys," as she motions her free hand towards the awaiting fairies.

"Well nice to meet you all!" Becca replies, taking Easter's offered hand and shaking it energetically.

"Yes, nice to meet you," Lizzie whispers while timidly shaking Easter's hand. "But what do you mean by OUR family?" she asks as she looks at me.

"Girls! THREE girls!" Mrs. Tiger cries happily, interrupting us and clapping her hands together excitedly. She has a look of absolute joy and astonishment on her face. My sisters and I turn towards her as she raves, "Oh, I love granddaughters! This is all so very, very exciting!" she gushes.

Leaning towards me, Lizzie whispers, "Should we be worried? What is she talking about?"

Becca leans towards us and asks, "I think the orange fairy is crazy. This goat is definitely crazy," she adds as she pushes Bubble Gum away from her. "I have a plan," Becca whispers. "Trust me."

Becca quickly pulls a long, striped sock from her pocket, rolls it into a ball, and throws it as hard and fast as far as she can. "Fetch!" she yells at Bubble Gum. Bubble Gum's head follows the sock up over her own head and she trips over her own legs as she jumps to catch it. Then missing the sock, she takes off after it.

Grabbing Lizzie and I by the arms, Becca screams at us, "RUN! Now is our chance!"

I am pulled off of my feet and land heavily on my butt.

No, I am definitely no fairy, I think in dismay, rubbing my throbbing butt cheek.

"Ouch!" I cry out to Becca. "Stop that!" I struggle as she tries to pull me up. "They are fairies!" I state in exasperation. "Do you think we can outrun them? Are we faster than them? And have you witnessed their magic? And where would we go? Do you know the way home?"

Still pulling on my arm, Becca replies, "We have to try. They sound crazy to me!"

Lizzie puts her free hand on Becca's shoulder and interjects, "Calm down, Becca. I agree with Ana."

"Oh, where are my manners? I am sorry, girls," Mrs. Tiger apologizes. "Allow me to explain," She flies closer to us and twirls a magnificent orange wand in a circle above us. The circle shimmers and glows, and our mother's face appears in the center of it. "Is this your mother?" Mrs. Tiger asks us.

"YES, that is our mom. Why?" Becca asks suspiciously.

Smiling hugely Mrs. Tiger replies, "I ask, my dear, because that is our daughter." The picture twirling in front of us zooms out to reveal more of our mom, and we scrutinize her odd silk purple dress. It is gorgeous, being shoulder less and slim fitting. It has yellow details around the top and swells out playfully around her legs. Her long black hair is braided, then piled atop her head and...she has WINGS.

"MUM!" Royal yells out loudly. "You NEVER told me that I had another sister!"

"What?" Lizzie snaps. "What is going on here?" she asks frantically looking around, and I note that her chin is quivering in fear.

Then I notice that in the chaos, Bubble Gum had snuck up next to Lizzie and is now smelling her book intently.

Keeping one goat eye on Lizzie, Bubble Gum cautiously takes a small lick of Lizzie's flower book. Her eyes light up, and I recognize that look of hunger in her eyes.

She quickly takes a large bite of the book before Lizzie lifts it up and out of her reach. Sighing in frustration, Bubble Gum picks up a sock covered with cartoon puppies from the ground and begins to eat it slowly. Never taking her eyes from Lizzie's book, she leisurely chews the sock, waiting for her opportunity.

Mr. Tiger steps up and puts a hand on Mrs. Tiger's shoulder. "We have a lot to talk about," he states simply.

"Yes, it is time that you all knew the truth," Mrs. Tiger agrees seriously.

Chapter Twenty-Nine - Forget Me

"We named our first-born child after the beautiful Nightshade Lily that was in bloom when she was born," Mrs. Tiger begins. "Night was a happy child, but before we knew it, she had grown up. We were busy running the Fairy Realm as Supreme Rulers, and Night had a lot of time to do as she pleased. When Royal and Stargazer were born, Night was terribly jealous of how much of our attention they took. Yes, she went from being the center of our universe to having to share us with two demanding babies," Mrs. Tiger adds. Smiling she turns to Royal and remembers, "You and Stargazer were wonderful babies," she reminisces. "But babies do take time."

"Odd things began occurring all over the Realm not long after Royal and Stargazer were born," Mr. Tiger explains. "Not just odd but evil things actually, and the Fairy folk were scared. There was a fairy using dark magic that went by the name Banshee, and we spent every spare moment trying to locate this Banshee."

I saw Easter wince at the name and remembered how desperate that other fairy at Pixie Palace was to hear that the Banshee wasn't back. *It must have been horrible, I think, for everyone to shudder at the name and dread the thought that this Banshee character was back.* I realized my mind had wandered and forced my attention back to Mrs. Tiger, who was talking now.

"It was a very stressful time," Mrs. Tiger was remarking.

"A tad more than just stressful, my dear," Mr. Tiger chimes in. "Banshee believed that Fairies should rule over all beings, and other Fairies began to agree with her. We started having uprisings and Fairies were arguing with other Fairies. I have never witnessed such discord and anger before," he finished sadly.

"All this trouble came from ONE ill-intentioned fairy, one greedy fairy who desired to have more. More power, more control. Banshee wanted more, and he would do anything to get it. Stirring trouble and putting Fairy against Fairy. Fairy against Leprechaun. Normally a Fairy wants what is best for their fellow creatures. We know that if all creatures are happy, all creatures will be in harmony, and the universe will flow as it should: peacefully. There is always a way for discussions that lead to compromise or consensus where everyone can agree on what is best. To try to take from one another. To try to force others to do what you want them to. That leads to anger and resentment, and that is the true evil," Mrs. Tiger said sadly.

"Night began spending more and more time away from us during this time. Then when we were about to capture Banshee, Night left us," Mr. Tiger states quietly.

Bursting into tears, Mrs. Tiger moans, "If she would have stayed for just a little bit longer, I am sure that everything would have worked out with Night and our search would have resulted in the capture of Banshee," Mrs. Tiger sobs. "We would have had more time for her again."

"What happened?" Royal asks, looking shocked.

"One morning we awoke, and the only thing that we could find of Night was a note written on a Nightshade petal," Mr. Tiger recalls sadly while hugging Mrs. Tiger tightly. "Most of her belongings were still in her room; it seemed like she would be right back, as if she were just staying at a friend's for a few days."

"What did the note say?" Lizzie asks curiously.

Sniffling, Mrs. Tiger responded, "The note said that she was in love with a NFF and had left the Fairy Realm to be with him. The note also asked us to not follow her, so we went to Moon Falls to at least catch a glimpse of her. We couldn't believe it. We had no idea that she had even met any NFFs, let alone fallen in love with one!"

"We were so busy. So distracted by everything else," Mrs. Tiger laments.

Shaking his head, Mr. Tiger elaborates, "The same day that Night disappeared, we began receiving complaints from fairy folk that they could not cross the meadow into the human realm. When she left, Night had closed off the Human World from ours. That is when we realized that Night was lost to us. We couldn't follow her, but we wanted to make sure that she was okay. So we asked Moon Falls to show her, but all that we could make out was static. It was the only time when Moon Falls would not allow us to view what we had requested."

"What happened to Banshee?" Lizzie asks curiously.

"We were too upset to continue our search for Banshee," Mrs. Tiger whispers sadly.

"No one has laid eyes on him since before Night left, so we assume that he escaped the Fairy Realm and went into hiding," Mr. Tiger reveals.

"But that is impossible," Royal interrupts. "Before today Moon Falls has ALWAYS shown what we ask. Why would it not?"

"What?" Mr. Tiger asks surprised. "What happened at the Falls today?"

"Haven't you been listening to any of the broadcasts?" Royal asks irritably.

"Oh, heavens, no, dear," Mrs. Tiger replies. "Now that we have passed on the ruler ship to you, we prefer to not try to stay current with the news."

"We keep up with things the old-fashioned way."

"Yes, we visit with fairies face to face. All of that news is so stressful anyway. To think of all of the different things that you have to manage by yourself."

"Yes, I do wish that you would take on co-ruler Royal. Give yourself a break from time to time," suggests Mr. Tiger.

"Dad," Royal replies affectionately. "I know that you mean well, but I am fine."

"Well a father is always concerned about his daughter," Mr. Tiger confesses lovingly. "But please tell us what happened at the Falls?"

Sighing, Royal admits, "Ana asked Moon Falls to show her grandparents today, and the Falls showed her you two."

Lizzie and Becca gasp in unison.

"It wasn't easy for the Falls," Royal admits. "And now it seems that the Falls is broken. There is a huge crack on its side, and it only shows static."

"Oh, dear," Mrs. Tiger whispers while looking away quickly.

"Mum," Royal asks suspiciously. "What do you know about this?"

"Oh, um. Well-you see…"

"And why can I not remember anything about Night?" Royal asks bewildered. "Even as small pixies, we fairies have very good memories."

"It is simple, my dear. We cast a Forget Me spell upon the entire Realm, so that everyone forgot about Night," Mr. Tiger mumbles, looking a little embarrassed.

Putting her hand to her head in shock, Royal insists, "But those spells are strictly forbidden!"

"Strictly forbidden for good reason," Mr. Tiger asserts. "We can't have fairies wiping away memories of other fairies!"

"But how could you perform the spell when it is STRICTLY forbidden?" Royal asks angrily.

"Well…strictly forbidden unless there is an extreme circumstance," Mrs. Tiger acknowledges.

"And that is at the discretion of the Supreme Rulers," Mr. Tiger maintains. "Which at the time were your mother and I."

"Is that why Moon Falls became damaged today?" Easter interrupts. "Because the memory that Ana was trying to view was hidden by the Forget Me spell?"

"I am afraid so," Mr. Tiger answers grimly.

"I KNEW we were right to ban that Forget Me spell!" Mrs. Tiger declares. "Look at the damage it has done! Why this is just terrible!"

"But, my dear," Mr. Tiger interrupts. "WE did the spell."

"Well that may be, but I still think it is a good thing that spell is forbidden! It is dangerous."

"I am sorry, my dear, I really am," Mrs. Tiger admits, looking at Royal. "You loved your big sister. But the Jays began attacking at the meadow, and it became so violent and so dangerous at the crossing that we did not want to risk you ever trying to find your sister. So we cast the Forget Me Spell on the entire Realm."

"We still hoped that Night would return to us one day," Mr. Tiger continues. "So we asked Night's best friend to be our Guardian at the crossing and to look for Night. He agreed to help her return if she ever came to the Meadow again."

"That explains why he let you three cross," Easter announces excitedly. "He knew that you were Night's daughters! Oh, this is all so exciting!"

"The horse is Night's best friend?" I ask skeptically, shooting a quick glance towards Bubble Gum.

Bubble Gum, who had been eating flowers, happily looked up and turned to face me.

"Does that surprise you?" Mrs. Tiger asks me. I know that NFFs generally cannot understand animals, but surely by now you have witnessed that we can."

Bubble Gum spits her flowers towards me disgustedly and walks to Easter's side.

"I, I am sorry," I stammer. "I didn't mean to offend anyone."

"But why didn't the Guardian report to you that Night's daughters were here?" Royal asks the Tigers.

"That is puzzling," agrees Mr. Tiger.

"Never mind about that," Mrs. Tiger dismisses while waving her hand. "We will ask him when we visit with him. The important thing is that our granddaughters found us!"

Mr. Tiger steps forward and embraces Royal, warmly declaring, "Indeed! We made sure to spend as much time with you and Stargazer as we possibly could after Night left. We didn't want to make the same mistake again."

Pulling her daughter in for a hug, Royal says, "And now we know why Mum always stressed how important family is. I have an older sister out there somewhere."

Chapter Thirty- Moon and Stars

Sighing, Mr. Tiger confesses quietly, "I am afraid that there is more."

"What do you mean?" Royal inquires.

"Well...after Night left, we discovered that she had taken our Moon Stone," reveals Mr. Tiger.

"What?" asks Becca. "What is a Moon Stone? And what does it have to do with anything?"

"Oh, I have examined those," Lizzie blurts out excitedly.

"What do you mean?" I quiz her. "Where have you seen Moon Stones?"

"When we became separated, I awoke to find myself surrounded by the biggest, brightest, closest stars I have ever observed. They spoke with me and then the moon joined us and–"

"WHAT!?" shouts Becca loudly. "Talking stars?" Then concern comes across her face, and lowering her voice, she softly asks, "Are you okay, Lizzie? Did you, um, maybe bump your head?"

"I am fine!" Lizzie shouts hotly. "What is so strange about stars and moons that can speak with you? You just spent your time with LEPRECHAUNS! LEPRECHAUNS, Becca! And we are currently having a discussion with flying fairies! All of this is strange!"

Taken aback by Lizzie's outburst, Becca takes a deep breath and then answers softly, "Okay, okay, Lizzie. I am sorry. It just sounds so strange. Did they have mouths I mean? How did they even talk to you?"

Crossing her arms, Lizzie regards Becca coolly for a moment before replying. "No, they didn't have mouths. The words were…they were just in my head. They didn't have to speak anything out loud, and I still knew what they were saying…"

Becca interrupts exasperatedly, "Oh, come now! You are just teasing us! Or maybe you did hit your head…HARD."

Before Lizzie could argue, Easter steps forward and proclaims, "I believe you, Lizzie." Then looking at the three of us, she reveals, "After you inhaled Passion's dust, you were separated by your strengths and placed with those who you would most closely relate to and feel comfortable with while you were being observed."

"B…being observed?" Becca asks.

"Yes, we had to know if you were dangerous to us or not, so we separated you from one another and study you. The moon and the stars see all and know all, so they advised where you should each be placed. They understood Lizzie to be a very intelligent and curious being and asked to analyze her themselves." Turning towards Becca, she clarifies, "You, on the other hand, were identified as a fun-loving prankster, so they placed you with the Leprechauns."

Why was I placed with Easter? I wonder. But before I can ask, Easter continues.

"Everything that Lizzie is claiming is true. Please listen to her." Then looking at Lizzie, she implores, "Please proceed, Lizzie."

Smiling softly at having Easter stand up for her and her incredible story, Lizzie clears her throat and explains. "As I was saying, when I woke up, I realized that the 'ground' that I was on was very soft and moved easily. It was gray and puffy looking. When I tried to stand, my feet sank, so that I could not make them out. I felt as if I were going to fall right through the strange, squishy floor. I started to panic when I heard voices. I called out for help, but I couldn't see anyone. So naturally I quieted down to make out the words. After a few moments, I could understand what they were describing."

"Who was it?" I asked anxiously. "What did you hear?"

"I didn't know at first," Lizzie admits. "All of this information began to fill my head. It was so much to take in that I wished I had a notebook. Once that thought entered my mind, I felt something in my hands and looked down to discover that I was holding the most beautiful notebook that I had ever seen.

This, THIS notebook," she announces loudly, holding up the delicate flower book in her hands for us to examine. "I began to analyze the notebook and I wondered if it was paper at all. Or instead maybe the flowers were fused together somehow to form a surface upon which to write. That's when I realized that I could hear the voices again in my head, and they were answering my questions. Somehow the voices could comprehend my thoughts. I wasted no time in wishing for a pen and voila!" she announces triumphantly. "This most impressive antique quill pen appeared in my hand. Look at that feather! That is a genuine peacock feather. On a quill! Just amazing!" she declares excitedly, holding the feather pen in front of her.

"Yes, it is a beautiful...pen," I repeat kindly. *Really it is gigantic, and I would probably poke myself in the eye with it*, I think.

"It is, isn't it?" Lizzie agrees admiringly. "Would you like to try it? All you do is tip the point into the jar of ink and then write until you need more ink. Like this," she demonstrates enthusiastically.

I quickly hold my hands up and back away. "Me? Use a jar of ink? You know me, Lizzie. That is nice of you, but you know I would just spill the ink and wreck your fancy quill and delicate book."

Lizzie pauses in mid demonstration. Then turning slightly pink, she nods. "Yes, I suppose so. Thank you for reminding me. Sorry. I got a little carried away."

Smiling I encourage her, "What happened after you got the quill?"

"Oh, yes. Well I quickly began asking questions. I started with who they were, and they told me that they were the stars. The clouds parted above me, and I could take in the lovely stars. They each had their own name, and the individual star would twinkle and grow brighter whenever I addressed them. Then the moon joined us, and he had loads to report! Oh, we talked about so many things! I had no idea that there was so much to learn!"

"Only you would study when you find a magical fairy land!" Becca exclaims sarcastically. "Incredible!"

"Becca," I warn. "Knock it off and LISTEN! Please. That is wonderful, Lizzie," I encourage. "But what did you say about the Moon Stones?"

"Oh, yes. I am sorry. There is so much to tell! Yes, they have many, many wondrous Moon Stones that they showed me. Each stone is a different color; there were blues and purples, pinks and greens and yellows to just name a few! They were different sizes depending upon how large their universe is."

"Their what?" inquires Becca.

"What? Oh, yes. The purpose of the Moon Stones is to protect universes. Each one has an entire universe encased inside its beautiful gem. If you looked closely, you could notice the stars twinkling in some. It was all quite marvelous really. The moon told me that it is their greatest responsibility to protect these precious stones and the delicate universes enclosed within them. It is a great responsibility, and he shamefully admitted that he was the destroyer of the dinosaurs when there was an unfortunate accident."

"What!?" screams Becca. "Do you have any idea how crazy that sounds?"

"I do, Becca. I was surprised by it myself when he told me." Facing me Lizzie whispers, "There was a sign with a large Tyrannosaurus Rex on it next to the Moon Stones that read 'Careful-Remember the Dinosaurs.'"

"Poor Moon still feels guilty over it," she divulges.

"Over killing off the dinosaurs?" Becca presses irritably. "That is crazy. How could he have done that anyway?"

"Didn't you learn anything while you were with the Leprechauns?" Lizzie asks annoyed.

"I learned more than you did!" Becca challenges. "We just didn't talk about rocks, that's all. There are many more important things to.....discuss," she trails off as she smiles in remembrance.

"Sure," Lizzie scoffs. "From what I saw, all you did was take a swim in old socks!"

"Did not! Take it back!"

"Not a chance," Lizzie declares, smiling sweetly.

"Girls, that is enough," Mr. Tiger commands, silencing them. "Allow me to explain to Becca. A while back," he begins, "dinosaurs did roam the Earth until the moon accidentally dropped one of the stones. He was polishing the stones when one slipped. The stone cracked, and enough cold air was allowed to enter the stone that it was referred to as the Ice Age."

Becca gasped, "No way! The moon did cause dinosaurs to be extinct. But that was so long ago. How could that be?"

"It wasn't that long ago to us," Mr. Tiger corrects sternly. "It was before our daughters were born, but I remember it clearly. There was pure panic and chaos in that galaxy."

"Most of the dinosaurs died as you know," Mrs. Tiger remarks. "But with disaster comes opportunity also."

"Yes, another species, humans, had the ability to thrive and grow without the larger, stronger dinosaurs to worry about."

"We helped the moon repair the crack before the entire universe was destroyed. Then as thanks, the moon entrusted the Fairy Realm with a single Moon Stone," Mr. Tiger states. "And Night took that very stone with her when she left."

"Needless to say, the moon was not pleased with us when he realized that she had taken a Moon Stone," Mrs. Tiger remarks grimly.

"Thankfully reports indicate that the universe within that gem has not suffered while in her care. Except for one instance where there were great earthquakes and storms that is. My guess is that she must have dropped it."

I gulp in nervousness at this and lower my eyes, remembering when I dropped Mother's charm. *Had I caused those disasters*, I wonder. I hope not. I sneak a glance at Easter and can tell that she is thinking the same thing that I am. And I know, I know that Mother's charm must indeed be a Moon Stone and that when I dropped it, I caused massive chaos in the tiny universe within it. *Oh, I feel awful*, I think.

Easter clears her throat and reveals, "Ana has viewed it."

Everyone turns to look at her in surprise, "What do you mean?" Royal asks.

"Ana's mom has a Moon Stone! I mean Ana described a good luck charm that her mom NEVER takes off, and it sounds like a Moon Stone. AND while Ana was holding it in her hands, it responded to her touch!"

"Do you mean to say that it twinkled?" Mrs. Tiger quizzes in disbelief.

"No, I mean, yes," Easter spits out excitedly. "It did more than twinkle, Grams! Ana saw a shooting star in it!"

Everyone turned to stare at Ana in astonishment. "Is that good?" Ana questions. Embarrassed by the way everyone is staring at her so intently.

"Night must have taken it as a precaution," Mr. Tiger mumbles thoughtfully, not answering me.

"What do you mean? Why is that?" Lizzie implores curiously.

Mr. Tiger murmurs, "A Moon Stone will grant the wish of any fairy that holds it in their hand." Looking at me, Mr. Tiger inquires, "What were you thinking when you saw the shooting star within the stone?"

Frowning, I try to remember. "Well...I suppose I was thinking of my grandparents. Mother said that her charm had come from her parents, but otherwise she does not talk about them, and I have always wondered..."

Realizing that the Tigers were Mother's parents, I look at them apologetically and stammer, "I mean. Um, I didn't mean anything bad. I–I–I don't know why she didn't talk about you. But I am sure it wasn't anything bad. I mean, um…"

Mr. Tiger raises his hand to silence me and remarks gently, "Never mind that, child. If she had talked to us, you may have figured out that we were fairies."

"So when you held the Moon Stone, you thought of us?" Mrs. Tiger insists quietly.

"Uh, um, yes. Yes, I did."

"Was that just before you found the fence?' she asks.

I can feel my eyes widen, and my jaw drops open in astonishment. "It was. Just a few days later, my sisters and I found the fence. I wished to know about you and that led us here, didn't it?"

Putting her hand on Mr. Tiger's arm, Mrs. Tiger smiles warmly at me and replies, "Yes, dear. Your wish brought you and your sisters here. Because of your wish, we are able to meet, and you now know that you are part of the Lily family. That you are a fairy."

Chapter Thirty- One - Now What

"What do we do know?" I ask in a shocked whisper.

Stepping forward Lizzie interrogates the Tigers, "If you did the original Forget Me spell, are you able to undo it?"

"Yes, yes. We can undo the Forget Me spell but then everyone would remember Night and that terrible Banshee. We have spent many years erasing those dark times from everyone's memories," Mrs. Tiger whispers softly.

"Along with the bad memories, you also caused everyone to forget their good memories from that time. Like my memories of my sister," Royal observes.

"But what if people try to cross over?" Mr. Tiger poses. "The Jays still attack at the crossing. And they support Banshee. It is still dangerous."

"The Meadow is still closed, so that no Fairy may cross over," Mrs. Tiger comments. "That would be revealed to all of the fairies along with everything else."

"I suppose if everyone knew that, they couldn't cross, and they already know that it is dangerous..." Mr. Tiger trails off thoughtfully.

"Maybe we could speak with Night," Mrs. Tiger whispers. She looks up at us, and there are tears in her eyes. "It has been a very long time, and we have missed so much. Look at these three lovely granddaughters that we never even knew about."

Clearing his throat solemnly, Mr. Tiger whispers tenderly, "But Night has requested us to not follow her. We have to honor that request. It is Fairy Law to honor requests of other fairies."

"Maybe she would allow the girls to learn their Fairy heritage and visit us. Maybe they could inform her that we are terribly sorry and that we love her," Mrs. Tiger suggests quietly. Looking at us, she asks, "Would you do that for me? For us?"

"Of course we would," I quickly agree. "We haven't even left yet, and I am already looking forward to coming back!"

"How about we just change that law?" Becca pipes in. "Sounds like a silly law anyway. And you could do it, couldn't you?" she implores Royal.

"Yes, dear, I could change that law. But no matter how much I would like to meet my sister again, I would not change that law. It is part of what makes us good and successful. Imagine if in the human realm when someone asked you to honor a request and you had to."

"Well that would be fun," Becca gushes. "I would have Lizzie to do all of my homework!"

Smiling, Royal continues, "But you would also be obligated to honor others. Thus if your teachers were to request you to do your own homework…"

"Oh," Becca replies sadly.

"It is showing each other the utmost respect," Mr. Tiger adds. "We wanted to ignore Night's request and follow her, but we would never do such a thing."

"The only requests that may be ignored are requests that would cause you to break one of the other Fairy Laws," Royal explains.

"There are more? What are the other laws?" Lizzie quizzes intrigued.

At this Easter steps forward, and putting both of her hands behind her back, she looks seriously towards the sky and begins to recite slowly:

To be a Fairy is a wondrous thing, and it is an honor to be able to abide by the following Fairy Laws:

* A Fairy shall never harm another Fairy, unless in self defense

* A Fairy shall care for and protect all Realms

* A Fairy shall always honor the requests of other Fairies

* All Fairies are not equal

* All Fairies have the right to bear wands

* Fairies shall respect the Distinguished Dignitaries-The Goats
* And the most important law—No Fairy shall fly upside down

Finishing Easter looks at us and grins.

"Thank you, my dear," Royal tells her.

"Those sound like interesting rules," Lizzie comments, "May I implore why there is no flying…"

"Not now, Lizzie," Becca interrupts her.

"Well how about the not all Fairies are equal rule? What does that mean?" Lizzie questions curiously.

"Lizzie!" Becca snaps. "No one cares right now! We have to figure out how to get home!"

Frowning, Lizzie picks up her quill and begins to write. "Well I will have to remember to find out more about the Governing of Fairies later then," she huffs. "Besides," she continues, "I don't know about you, but I like it here. I am in no hurry to get home."

"I like it here, too," I agree. "But Becca is right, we have to get home. Mom and Dad are probably worried sick by now."

Waving her hand, Mrs. Tiger dismisses, "That is nothing to worry about."

"What do you mean?" Becca demands her.

"Fairy Time is different than time in your realm," Easter volunteers helpfully. "How long have you been here?" she quizzes us.

"Um, a few days I think," I say trying to remember. *When had I last slept*, I think. I remember sleeping in the Fairy Fort, but have I since then? What about food? When had I last eaten? I remember eating that delicious cookie from Salvia, but nothing other than some tea since then. Why am I not hungry?

Becca interrupts my thoughts, "I don't know how long we have been here," she admits. "It doesn't make any sense. It seems like we have been here for days and days, but I don't remember sleeping or eating or even the sun setting."

"Before you entered another Realm and became our size, you slept and ate like you had before," Easter comments, "Upon entering the Fairy Realm, you entered Fairy Time. That is why we are so much older than humans yet we appear young."

"In your realm, only minutes have passed since you crossed the meadow and went behind the waterfall," Royal explains.

My mouth falls open. "Min...min...minutes?" I ask dumbly. "Do you mean that Mom and Dad..."

"They probably don't even know that you are missing," Royal speculates.

Chapter Thirty-Two - Goodbye

"That may be," Mrs. Tiger agrees. "But they are still Non-Fairy Folks."

"HALF NFFs," Easter interrupts.

"Yes, my dear. They are half NFF. But we still shouldn't keep them here much longer."

"Why is that?" Lizzie questions.

"Though you may not feel a need to sleep or eat while in the Fairy Realm, it will all come to you once you reenter the Human Realm," Mr. Tiger explains. "If you have been here for twenty-four Fairy hours, once you return, you will feel exhausted and starving."

"Yes, your body realizes that it has been operating without breaks or nutrition. Once you return, your body will need to replace all that it missed," Mrs. Tiger cries.

"Oh, dear!" Royal declares. "With all of the excitement, I had forgotten about that. Yes, we had better hurry in order to avoid another unpleasant situation."

"What do you mean by that?" Lizzie demands, looking alarmed.

"Oh, it is nothing. Nothing to worry about, my dear. Let's just hurry." Royal commands urgently.

"Are you talking about the NFF who perished?" Easter whispers to her mom.

"PERISHED?" Becca shrieks. "As in dead?"

"Oh, I am sure it hasn't been that long yet," Royal comments reassuringly. "Really there is nothing to worry about."

Looking towards us, Easter explains, "Once there was a human who stayed in our realm for too long, and when they returned to their world, they had missed too much food and too much sleep. They couldn't handle it. They just collapsed and died on the edge of the meadow."

I gasped, and I must have looked horrible because Easter rushes towards me and takes my arm. Looking me in the eye, she says, "I am sure that it will be fine. You surely haven't been here that long. Mum, how long had that NFF been with us?"

"Seventy-five hours," Royal replies quietly.

"And how long has Ana and her sisters been with us?"

"Seventy-three hours by my calculations," Royal responds quietly.

Hearing this Easter's face tightens, and her smile falters for a moment. Then she pulls herself together and declares brightly, "See! We still have two more hours! Nothing to worry about!"

"I feel sick," Lizzie mumbles, sitting down.

"WE ARE GOING TO DIE!" Becca screams hysterically and begins to cry. "I am too young to die! You, two!" She yells, pointing at Lizzie and I. "You two have lived your life! You are years older than me. But I am so young!"

"Thanks a lot," I yell angrily to Becca.

"Let's not fight," Mrs. Tiger commands sternly to us. Looking at the other fairies, she pleads, "Let's just help these girls cross back to their realm before anyone gets hurt. And they are half fairy, so who knows how long they have."

"I really don't want to find out how long we have," Lizzie confesses seriously. "Now I just want to go home."

"That is exactly where we will take you," Royal promises calmly. Pulling her long elegant wand out, she lifts it above her head and calls out, "Let's do this, everyone, let's send these girls home!"

The Tigers, Royal, Easter, and Bubble Gum gather around us. They encircle us and raise their wands above our heads.

"I had a lot of fun with you," Easter announces smiling.

"Please come back to visit, my dears," Mr. Tiger implores.

"Please HURRY back," Mrs. Tiger requests.

"Tell the Leprechauns thank you and that I will miss them," Becca calls out.

"Thank you for everything that you have taught me," Lizzie thanks them.

"Baa," screeches Bubble Gum, trying for one last nibble on Lizzie's book.

"We will be back as soon as we can," I cry out to them. "Thank you for everything."

I feel something on my hair and look up to notice glitter showering from their wands onto us. Sparkling orange, glittering clear white, and shiny pink softly falls onto us. It feels like snow, except it is warm and each piece makes me feel good when it touches my skin. Almost like a kiss. It makes me feel loved. I shut my eyes against the warmth, against the love, against the magic. I wonder what I will see when I open my eyes.

Chapter Thirty-Three - Home

I hear water rushing, and the air feels damp. Taking a deep breath, I open my eyes to realize that I am just behind the waterfall. Lizzie and Becca are next to me, and I hug them tightly

"Are you alright?" I ask them. "How do you feel?"

"So far I feel fine. But I will miss them all. I will miss them dearly," Lizzie admits. "Does that make me a bad person?"

"If it does, then I am a bad person, too," Becca replies. "I am going to miss them A LOT!" she declares dramatically.

Smiling, I say, "Me, too. But we will go back again."

"Yes," Lizzie answers. "After we have a very long conversation with Mother. I have so many questions."

"I do, too," I agree as we carefully step from behind the waterfall into the meadow where it all began. My stomach rumbles, and we look at each other giggling. "I am hungry, but other than that, I feel fine!" I exclaim happily with relief.

"Me, too!" Becca declares. "They made me nervous with all of that talk about dying from hunger and starvation. Phooey, they must have been exaggerating!"

"You looked more than nervous," Lizzie states matter of factly. "You were panicking, downright hysterical."

"I was not!"

"Come on, you two!" I shout at them. "Stop arguing," but I am smiling in relief.

"You are right," Lizzie states. "Maybe we are Fairies because other than being hungry, I feel great! We must get home and interrogate Mother about all of this."

"And Dad," Becca adds. "Do you think Dad knows?" We look at each other silently. "He must," Lizzie starts.

"He can't," I declare at the same time.

We look at each other and giggle nervously. "Let's find out," suggests Becca. "Race you home!" and with that, she takes off in a fast run.

Lizzie and I look at each other, then race after her. I trip over my feet and almost fall on the soft grass as we run towards the fence. I am the slowest, and my feet clumsily pound the ground as I attempt to catch up with my sisters. As I gracelessly stumble towards home, I think, *I can't possibly be related to those dainty, elegant, perfect fairies...can I?*

If you loved this book please rate or review it. Follow me on Amazon, Good-reads or www.edevoldbooks.com to be notified when the next book in *The Other Side of the Fence* series is available.

"You can find magic wherever you look, sit back and relax, all you need is a book."

Dr. Seuss